W9-BEU-828

THE LOST ISLAND

THE LOST ISLAND

EILÍS DILLON

Illustrated by

RICHARD KENNEDY

THE NEW YORK REVIEW CHILDREN'S COLLECTION

New York

THIS IS A NEW YORK REVIEW BOOK
PUBLISHED BY THE NEW YORK REVIEW OF BOOKS
1755 Broadway, New York, NY 10019
www.nyrb.com

This edition published by agreement with The O'Brien Press Ltd., Dublin
First published by Faber and Faber Ltd., London, 1952
First published by The O'Brien Press Ltd., 1986

Library of Congress Cataloging-in-Publication Data
Dillon, Eilís, 1920–
The lost island / by Eilís Dillon.
p. cm. — (New York Review children's collection)
Summary: When a tramp brings what may be a message from his missing father, Michael determines to follow the piecemeal clues and find a boat and crew for the hazardous journey in search of an unknown island located somewhere off the coast of western Ireland.
ISBN 1-59017-205-1 (alk. paper)
[1. Adventure and adventurers—Fiction. 2. Missing persons—Fiction. 3. Islands—Fiction. 4. Ireland—Social life and customs—20th century—Fiction. 5. Mystery and detective stories.] I. Title. II. Series.
PZ7.D5792Lo 2006
[Fic]—dc22
2006009939

ISBN-13: 978-1-59017-205-6
ISBN-10: 1-59017-205-1

Cover design by Louise Fili Ltd.

Printed in the United States on acid-free paper.
1 3 5 7 9 10 8 6 4 2

For

EILÉAN AND MÁIRE

★ I ★

This adventure really began one early spring morning when I was fourteen years old. I remember it all so clearly, from the moment when I stepped out into the still dark yard and went to unlock the stable door. The pony whinnied very quietly and stirred his feet in the straw of his bed. I remember looking up at the stars. Soon a soft light would come from the east, so gently that it would hardly be noticed at first. Then the birds would stir, and suddenly it would be day and the stars gone. I had always loved these early mornings when the pony and I travelled along in warm companionship to the Saturday market in the town.

I opened the door and the pony nuzzled my coat in friendliness. I led him out and harnessed him there in the starlit yard. Then we clopped over to the cart-shed where the cart was waiting with its shafts in the air. It was already loaded from the night before. There were orange-coloured carrots with their tails tied in bundles. There were turnips and onions and crisp curly cabbages. There was a wooden keg of buttermilk bound with iron hoops. Then just as I was ready to go, my mother came out of the house with two long deep covered baskets. One had eggs and a roll of butter wrapped in muslin, and the second had a pair of fat young cocks. They poked their beaks through a hole in the basket and glared, but they lay there quietly enough, with their feet bound with red tape.

DWYER
JAMES

MICHAEL CASSIDY

Then I called to the pony and chucked at the reins and we were off, slowly through the yard and down the lane, and faster when we came to the smoother road outside.

Soon it was broad daylight. The cottage doors began to open, and a crowd of starving hens shrieked before each. Thin grey smoke went up straight from the chimneys and sheep-dogs came out of the houses to lie in the sun. The pony trotted along comfortably with his mind on the business of getting us to town, except when he whinnied a greeting to one of his friends in a field by the roadside.

Presently we caught up with a stream of carts. Mountainous old women in patterned fawn-coloured shawls sat in the donkey-carts. The donkeys dragged them along patiently, with their ears down, thinking the long sad thoughts of all donkeys. The men were driving big horse-carts, some with high loads of turf, thatched on the top to keep them dry. The yellow spring sunlight cast our shadows on the roadside as we moved along companionably together.

There was already a great bustle in the town when we arrived, although it was still quite early. On the square little pens had been made of the creels of carts, to hold calves and sheep and young pigs. Loud bargains were being made and money was changing hands. The animals were crouching in their pens, looking rather frightened, I thought. The tinkers were there, of course, with their thimble-men and trick-of-the-loop men, but they were doing no business yet.

I drove straight to the vegetable market, where I soon found a good stand. I loosened the traces and tilted the cart backwards to show what I had to sell, and then I gave the pony some oats in a nosebag hitched around his ears. Then there was no more to be done except wait for customers, and look about to see who was there.

A little apart from the vegetable carts the china-seller

had laid out a long row of cups and saucers, plates, bowls and earthenware of all kinds. He was standing behind them, a little man like a weasel, bawling to the crowd in a voice much too powerful for his size.

"Great bargains, ladies and gentlemen! Here's a bowl that cost me a shilling, but I'm willing to sell it for tenpence. Who'll give me tenpence for this bowl?"

He held it up, and a woman in the crowd said:

"Ninepence!"

The china-seller stopped, outraged.

"Did ye all hear what she said? Ninepence! Ninepence for that beautiful bowl, that unique bowl, that cost me a silver shilling!" He turned to the woman, with the bowl raised in his two hands. "Rather than sell it for ninepence, ma'am, I'll smash it to atoms!"

He sent the bowl crashing on to the pavement. A horrified shiver went through the crowd. The woman called out:

"Oh, why did you do that? Oh, glory to Heaven, the lovely bowl!"

"I'll smash every one of them before I'll sell them for ninepence," said the china-seller fiercely.

"Ah, now, sir, don't do that at all," said the woman hurriedly. "Look now, alanna, I'll buy one from you for tenpence. Sure, 'tis a fine bowl, 'tis indeed, and good value for the money. And I'm sure you'll sell the rest of them, too, sir."

The crowd needed no more persuasion, and the china-seller began to hand out his little stock of bowls to the cheerful chink of tenpences going into his pocket. While his hands worked busily he had time to notice that I was watching him, and he gave me a brief, sly wink.

It was then I saw a boy of about my own age standing at the edge of the crowd. He was smaller than me, and much thinner, and he had big dark-brown eyes like bog-holes, full of amusement now as he watched how the china-seller had tricked the crowd. He came over in a friendly way and rubbed my pony's nose.

"What do you call him?"

"Mulcahy," said I. "The servant of war, you know. I'm sure he would have been a war-horse if he had been bigger and had been born a few hundred years ago."

"Do you really own him? Yourself, I mean?"

"We have a farm," I explained. "Since my father went away four years ago, I've been trying to work it for my mother. So I suppose you could say I own Mulcahy, and all the other animals too."

"I have some animals," he said. "Not a horse, of course. Would you like to see them?"

He collected a handful of the pony's mane and ran it lovingly through his fingers.

I agreed readily to go with him, but said I must sell my vegetables first. He said he would wait for me, and he stood there watching me through the long morning until I was finished. Then I harnessed the pony again and we sat on the cart and drove down towards the docks. Joe Clancy was his name, he said, and he asked for mine. When I told him he repeated it over and over:

"Michael Farrell, Michael Farrell—that suits you."

Joe had a kind of nest made from an enormous wooden crate right on the dock, but a little back from the water. He lifted away the wooden door. We went in, and I looked around in astonishment. Against the walls he had made cages of laths and odd bits of wire, and in these he had collected as queer an assortment of small creatures as you could hope to see. There were two rabbits and a small mongrel dog, a seagull and a jackdaw, and what looked to me like a stout water-rat in the dimness at the back.

"They all have something wrong with them," Joe explained. "The rabbits both have broken legs, and the seagull has a broken wing. The jackdaw is to young too fly —he was blown out of someone's chimney, I suppose. The rat—well, I think he's only pretending, but then people always think the worst of rats, they're so shifty-looking."

Indeed that rat was the sleekest, smoothest, most comfortable-looking rat I had ever seen. He sat back on his hunkers in his cage, looking cheerfully pleased with himself. Joe's conscience need not have pricked him for suspecting him of dishonesty.

"And here's a fellow I never had before," said Joe proudly, opening a box near the rat's cage. "Peep in at him carefully—he's very frightened."

I looked in, and there was a small red squirrel cowering in one corner. He looked up at us miserably and looked away again.

"I wish I could bandage his paw," said Joe, "but he's so nervous that he bites every time I touch him."

"Perhaps he smells the rat," I suggested. "I'm sure they would not be friends."

I privately thought it unlikely that that rat had any friends. He looked like a small wicked pirate.

"Rats and squirrels are related to each other, in a way," said Joe. "But still, I'll move his box away from the rat and see if that will make him happier."

He lifted the box and set it down nearer the door. Then we looked into it again. This time the squirrel looked up at us for longer, though he still seemed frightened.

"We'll have to give him time," said Joe. "If he doesn't improve soon I'll have to let him go."

We went out into the sun again, and Joe told me something about himself. He was an orphan, but he had been taken in by a fisherman and his wife when he was very young. He lived with them still, in a cottage down by the docks.

"It'll be dinner-time now," he said. "Come on home with me."

I hesitated for a moment. In the years since my father had gone away, and I was trying to help my mother to manage our farm, I had learned many a bitter lesson. I knew that a person that wants a favour is never as welcome as one who brings a present. I knew too that since I lived the life of a grown man, with very little time for play, I must learn to think and act like a grown man also.

"Perhaps they won't want to have a stranger coming in to dinner," I said.

"That's not their way at all," said Joe. "Pete always says he likes a full house, and Mrs. Pete always puts a few extra potatoes in the pot, in the hope that someone will come to eat them. Ah, come on," he said persuasively, and started across the footbridge that ran along the top of the lock gates.

I did not want to refuse, so I followed him over the bridge. I longed for friends more than anything else at that time. Both my father and my mother were strangers to the place, so that I knew scarcely anyone in the town. But as soon as I followed Joe into Pete's kitchen, I knew at once that I need never have doubted my welcome.

The kitchen had an earthen floor, and you went down two steps into it from the path outside. An open fireplace almost filled the right-hand wall, and a three-legged pot hung over the big turf fire. Clouds of steam kept bobbing the lid up and down and the water gurgled and laughed around the potatoes in the pot. A delicious smell of cooking filled the room. The kitchen table had been pulled out from the wall, and knives and forks were set on the apple-patterned oilcloth. The firelight danced on the lustreware and rosy cups on the dresser, and I could well believe that this was a house where strangers were always welcomed.

As we came into the kitchen—I had to stoop my head

under the lintel—a woman rose up from the fireside where she had been watching a pan full of sizzling herrings. She was small and light and cheerful looking, though she was not young. She wore the long red skirt and crossed-over plaid shawl that all the fishermen's wives wore in those days. Her feet were bare.

"Mrs. Pete, I've brought Michael Farrell home for dinner," said Joe, displaying me proudly.

"You're heartily welcome," said Mrs. Pete. "Sit over there by the fire while I finish the dinner. Was the market good? I'm glad you came now, for I love to hear about the market when I don't have time to go myself. Joe doesn't see the right things."

Thus she made me feel that I had done her a favour by coming to eat her dinner. I spent the next few minutes in telling her who was at the market, and how the prices went, and how Johnny the China made the people buy the bowls.

"That's an old trick of his, and still the people are always surprised at it," she said, and added thoughtfully: "But do you know, 'tis an awful thing to see the lovely china smashed on the ground for the pigeons to be walking on it. Often I bought something from him to stop him from breaking more, for he'd really go on doing it until someone would start the ball rolling."

While we were talking Pete came into the kitchen. He was a big shambling man who always seemed to move carefully, as if he were afraid of knocking things over. But he could mend a net or bait a hook as neatly as any man in the place. He was dressed in a blue fisherman's jersey and homespun trousers. He had been cleaning his boat, which he always did on Saturdays, and now he washed his hands in a tin basin on top of a box behind the kitchen door. Then he came over and pulled out a chair from the table and sat down to wait for dinner.

Mrs. Pete strained the potatoes through a flat hazel

basket, and set the basket, steaming mightily, on the table. She put a juicy fat herring in front of each of us, and at last sat down herself at the head of the table.

"The blessing of God on us all," said Pete, and he selected a potato carefully from the basket.

While we were eating I had to tell them all about myself and about our farm.

"We had some very bad luck at first," I said. "We had a man who cheated us, and we thought we would have to sell out. And just at the right time along came old Billy. Daft Billy, the neighbours call him, because he talks to the animals. But we know he's not daft, and they're glad enough to call him when their own animals are sick. He had a farm of his own once, but for some reason he sold it and went out to work as a labourer on other people's farms. He was lonely, he said, and he has a little bit of money put away for his old age. I wish I knew as much about farming as Billy does."

"You have a long life to learn it in," said Pete. "And tell me now, why did your father go away?"

"I don't exactly know," I said. "My mother will never talk about it. I remember him coming home once in a state of great excitement, and then there was a long time when he seemed to be preparing for a journey, and there was talk of a boat. Then one morning when I got up—he was gone."

"That's a queer story," said Pete. "Have you never heard from him since?"

"Never. At first my mother didn't seem to expect any news, but now she spends all the time she can looking up and down the road. She won't ever tell me what she's watching for, though I've asked her many and many a time."

"That's a queer story indeed," said Pete thoughtfully, "and four years is a long time."

As soon as we had finished our meal Pete said:

"May He who gave us this good meal give us eternal life, Amen."

Then he lit his pipe and took a few comfortable pulls.

"Come away out and see the old boat, Michael," he said then, and we went out into the sunshine.

Right in front of us, Pete's boat was tied with the others against the quay wall. The tide was low, and only the masts showed. As it was Saturday no one was out fishing, and the boats were two and three deep against the wall. As we stood watching, other men came out of their houses after dinner and began to climb across the boats until each man reached his own. They sat there smoking, and calling to each other companionably in the sun. There were heaps of nets on the decks, and soon they began slowly to go over each one, looking for holes.

"Do you know anything about boats, Michael?" asked Pete.

"Nothing at all," I said. "I have never been in a boat."

Joe stared at me.

"And you living so near the sea!"

"My father was always down here on the quays," I said, "but my mother would never let me go with him. She said she was afraid of the sea."

I looked longingly at the black tarry boats, with their decks dark with age and their stout and capable-looking masts pointing at the sky.

"Come along down," said Pete decisively. "A boy of your age should know all about boats."

He went down a little iron ladder fixed against the quay wall and stepped into his boat. I followed and looked about me breathlessly. Here at last was one of my favourite dreams fulfilled. For as I went about my work at home I often amused myself by sailing in imagination across perilous seas, in just such a boat as this, on wild adventures. A boat like this Saint Brendan the Navigator had, when he sailed out alone across the Atlantic Ocean and discovered a new continent, as the stories said. This could have been the boat of O'Neill, the pirate, who brought home cargoes of loot from the high seas and ran them in by moonlight to the old quays, until they caught him and put him in gaol, and burned his boat out in the bay with all its load, like a beacon warning to others of his kind. And perhaps it was in a boat like this that my own father had sailed away four years ago, on what adventures I did not know. A little wild shiver ran up through me as I felt the water lifting the boat gently in a slow easy rhythm.

"There's nothing in the world as good as a good boat," said Pete.

"Come down below", said Joe, "and see the rest of her."

He disappeared through a square hatchway in the deck, so small that I thought Pete must have a tight squeeze to get through. But he slipped through easily and I followed him down a little wooden ladder into the hold. The smell of ancient fish made me gasp for air at first. Here the cargo of fish was always stored on the way home, and though the boat was cleaned after it was emptied, the smell seemed to have soaked into the timbers until it would have been impossible to have got rid of it. Pete and Joe did not seem to notice anything, so I kept quiet and hoped I would soon get used to it. A little shaft of light came down the hatchway and I could make out the stout timber ribs and long curved planks of the sides.

"This boat is a hundred years old," said Pete. "My great-grandfather built her with his own hands. He used to use her for carrying turf to the islands, but now she's mostly used for fishing. As fine a boat as you'll find in the bay, and as good as the day she was built. I wouldn't sell her for all the gold in Ireland."

Almost at the foot of the ladder there was an old rusty

tin can punched with holes towards the top. Pete explained that a turf fire was lit in this for boiling potatoes or water for tea when they were at sea. Sure enough, when we came on deck again I could see a thin stream of smoke coming from the hatches of some of the other boats.

"Those are the island boats," Pete explained. "The men live on them when they come into the town."

I had often seen the islandmen in the town on market days. They were always dressed in dark-blue homespun, and the raw-hide shoes that they made at home. They moved about and conducted their business with quiet dignity, and kept rather to themselves.

"Have you ever been to the islands?" I asked.

"Many and many a time," said Pete. "I have some very good friends there."

The three islands lay across the mouth of the bay. On a clear day they could be seen from the town, floating dimly on the horizon. They looked like the world's end, and it seemed impossible that people like myself should be living on them.

"I often wondered if it was to the islands that my father went," I said. "They say there are caves there that no one knows about, where a man could be in hiding for years."

Pete shook his head.

"A mainlander wouldn't know where those caves are," he said, "but you can be sure that the islanders know. And why would your father go into hiding? He had done nothing wrong."

"Of course not," I said. "But perhaps he had an enemy. I've thought about it all so much that I have no ideas left. If I had any clue about it all, I'd go after it and follow it up until I found him—alive or dead."

Joe said:

"And I'd go with you."

There was silence for a while. Then Pete said:

"I'm sure he's still alive. If he were not, you wouldn't feel this need to go and find him."

"Do you believe that?" I asked eagerly. "That is what I think myself. Oh, if only I had one word from him!"

We spoke no more about it. I had never told anyone how little I knew about my father's disappearance, but Pete and Joe were so friendly that I was glad to feel able to talk to them about it all.

We stayed on the boat for a while until I said that I must buy some things in the town before starting for home. We went back to the cottage and Mrs. Pete gave me some scones of her own baking, hot from the pot-oven on the hearth. She made me promise to come again on the next market day, and she waved to me from the door as I crossed the little footbridge over the lock again.

Joe came with me, with his pockets full of provisions for his animals. He fed them all carefully, each with what he thought it would like best. The rat had a whole scone which Mrs. Pete had given to Joe for himself.

"I like to give him the best things," said Joe as he watched the rat guzzle the scone. "I'd like to make it up to him for not being as nice as the other animals."

You should have seen that rat's face when he heard this. I thought he must count himself the happiest rat in the county.

My pony had waited patiently for me all this time, tethered to an old rusting buoy. I rubbed his nose and gave him a handful of oats before climbing into the cart. As I drove off, I called to Joe that I would see him on the next day that I would be in town.

It was late afternoon by now, and I had to hurry through my shopping. I wanted to be home in time for our evening meal, and besides I was eager to tell my mother about my new friends. As I left the town I passed a little file of donkey-carts starting on their slow way home. The fat old women woke from their doze to wave to me as the pony trotted briskly past. He smelled the stable, as the saying is, and was as anxious to get home as I was. Presently he tired a little, and settled down to a steadier trot. I let the reins go slack while I went over in my mind the happenings of the day.

After about three miles the dusk began to fall. We were on a bleak high stretch of the road now, with marsh and bog on either side. The pony started from time to time, as he caught sight of a white stone or a lone bush waving in the wind. I tightened my grip on the reins and spoke to him softly, for he was always nervous here at dark. He became quieter then, though he had quickened his pace.

Now we came to where a side road branched off into the bog. There was a low grassy bank by the roadside at the corner, and lying on it was what I took to be a heap of fluttering rags. But just as we were passing by it rose up on long legs and waved its ragged arms, while it uttered a terrible wailing cry. The pony shied across the road. I jerked at the reins and kept him clear of the banks by sheer force. Then he put his head back and fairly bolted, his galloping hooves thundering on the road. I clenched my teeth and held him in as best I could, but we had gone a mile before he began to slow down. He was in a lather of sweat, and froth dripped from his mouth. Still I did not try to stop him, for I was afraid he would take cold. I thought the best thing to do was to get him home to his warm stable, where Billy would give him a rub-down.

Now I had time to think of what had happened. Some tramp had been waiting by the roadside for the people coming from market, I supposed. When he saw me alone, he had perhaps intended to rob me, and had frightened the pony in the hope that I would be thrown from the cart, when I would be at his mercy.

It was quite dark by now, and to tell the truth, my heart

was still pounding with fright. I watched eagerly for the lights of our house, and when they came into view I almost cried with relief. At last I turned the pony into the lane, and a moment later pulled up at the kitchen door.

★ II ★

My mother had heard the pony's hooves on the cobbled yard, and she opened the kitchen door and came out. At the same time Billy came from the byre where he had been finishing off the milking. My mother took one look at the shivering pony and said:

"What happened?"

Her voice was husky with fright.

"The pony bolted," I said, trying to sound cooler than I felt. "A tramp shouted from the roadside and frightened him. It was that bleak place he doesn't like."

Billy patted the pony.

"He'll be all right. I'll give him a rub-down and tell him to forget about it."

He started to unharness the pony. My mother saw that I was unhurt, and said no more. She took some of her parcels off the cart and carried them into the kitchen, while I followed with the rest. Then she had to make sure that I had brought her the right things—thread and needles, oilcloth for the shelves, a special kind of wool for my own socks—oh, I was an expert on all these things! She seemed more cheerful than usual, and it gladdened my heart to see her smile.

Then it was time for our meal. I went out to the stable for Billy, for of course all three of us always sat down together, as was the good custom then, and still is. I found him in the stable, grooming the pony.

"He'll be all right now," he said, surveying the newly-smoothed coat. "I told him he should be long past such foolishness. He might have broken his leg—or even yours," he added with a grin.

He wiped his boots and washed his face and hands carefully before coming into the kitchen, for he was as dainty as a woman in his habits. During the meal I told them about Joe and Pete and Mrs. Pete, but I did not say that I had talked about my father.

After we had finished and had cleared away the things, we sat at the fire for a long time. Billy got his old pipe going, and settled himself comfortably in his chair. Then he began:

"I once met a man who had been to the island of Madagascar . . ."

This was what I loved. I had not got half the schooling I craved, but Billy's evening discourses were a splendid substitute. He would begin, as he did to-night, by mentioning some far-off part of the globe, and would then give a startlingly clear picture of it. He would describe the people, their dress and habits, their food, their religions and their history, with its relation to other countries, in close and accurate detail. Sometimes he would say:

"I have a little book about it, and I'll lend it to you."

This was a solemn honour. He would get up and go into his room, and come back with the book in his hand. Usually it was old and well-used. Then he would tell me about the book and its author and point me out the best passages. Later he would question me closely about it all, and encourage me to disagree with its opinions. In this way I had read a fair number of the world's classics, and had conceived a fine respect for books, partly from noticing the reverence with which Billy handled them.

My mother always listened to Billy's lectures too, while she sewed by the fire. I think it pleased her very much that

I was not to grow up ignorant, as I might easily have done.

On this night, it was quite late and the fire was beginning to die down when we were surprised to hear a knock at the door. It was unusual for our neighbours to be about so late. Billy said:

"Perhaps it's Pat Quinn. His cow was sick this morning."

I went to the door and opened it a piece. It was a pitch-dark and cloudy night with a promise of rain. There was no one on the doorstep, and I was puzzled for a moment. Then from one side a figure darted forward, a long lean figure in fluttering rags, and slipped past me into the kitchen.

My mother rose from her chair with a little scream. Billy started forward and stood between her and our visitor. I closed the door. By the flickering lamplight I had recognized him. It was the tramp who had frightened my pony that very afternoon.

"That was a bad trick you played on me to-day," I said.

He leered at me with his head slightly on one side. His cunning little eyes, with their red rims, flicked quickly about the room, rested on Billy's threatening attitude, and came back to me. He spoke in the high whining tone of the professional beggar.

"Ah, now, don't be hard on me, young fellow. No one minds poor old Mikus. Everyone knows me—Mikus Kavanagh—a decent man's son, that never did no one no harm."

"You could have killed me to-day," I said, for I was still boiling with anger at the meanness of his action.

"A clever young lad like you! You were in no danger. I was only going to ask you for a little information, yes, a little information. And if God saw fit to soften your heart —a little alms. That was all. No one minds poor Mikus."

He edged nearer to the fire, rubbing his claw-like hands together. My mother pulled forward her own chair.

"If you will sit down and warm yourself", she said, "I'll make you a cup of tea."

He started back in mock admiration, horrible to watch.

"A gracious lady, a fine lady, a noble lady!" He raised his voice to a whine again: "Thank you, thank you, ma'am, and may the blessings of heaven shower down on you and reward you for your goodness to the poor."

He pulled the chair briskly nearer to the fire and sat in it, leering triumphantly at me and at Billy in turn.

My mother busied herself making the tea. This did not surprise me, for it was her habit to feed and help any beggarman who called at our door. Often I noticed that the more unpleasant they were, the more she gave them.

Mikus mouthed to himself and rubbed his hands and hitched his chair closer and closer to the fire while he waited. Billy took down a piece of harness and became very busy at mending it, although it was now time for his nightly securing of doors and gates. The beggarman took no further notice of us, and when his tea was ready he drank it noisily and wolfed the soda-bread that my mother gave him with it. When he had finished he whined some more about her goodness and generosity, and the wealth of his language surprised me. He was not one of our regular beggarmen. There were four or five of these, who walked from one farmhouse to another from year's end to year's end, and came for a meal to our house every few weeks. Nor was he known in the neighbourhood, for we should surely have heard of such a strange character.

Billy said, without lifting his head from his work:

"You were not always a poor man, I'm thinking."

"No," said Mikus. "No." He paused a long time, looking into the fire. Then he said, in a tone that was almost normal, "I was a school teacher once, in a place a long way from here. It was a pleasant place, though very quiet. I had a good little house—I used to thatch it myself, and whitewash it twice a year."

He fell silent again.

"And what happened?" asked Billy.

Mikus jumped up in a sudden rage, and began to stride up and down the room.

"What happened? My neighbours began to talk, in whispers at first, soft, wicked little whispers. I used to hear them go hiss, hiss, whenever I passed by. Then they began to look in through my windows, yellow evil faces at my windows. Then they stopped whispering and began to shout at me—terrible things. They were not so perfect themselves—they were bad, bad, bad!"

His voice rose to a scream. None of us moved. Then Billy said:

"So you left that place?"

Mikus lowered his voice as he said:

"Yes. I left that place, my house and my school and my saintly neighbours. That was long ago."

He dropped wearily into the chair by the fire. My mother said:

"Have you a place to sleep to-night?"

A cunning look came into his face.

"I think I have. I have a message for some people who live about here, and when they get it they'll be so grateful that they'll surely give me a night's lodging. That was all I wanted of you this afternoon, young man, to know where Mrs. Farrell lives."

My mother started. She said urgently:

"I am Mrs. Farrell. What is the message?"

Mikus got up and bowed with ceremony.

"Madam, your servant! I never thought of that."

"The message," said my mother. "The message!"

He leered at her and began again in his hateful whine:

"Ah, now, don't be hard on a poor man that wishes you no harm."

"What do you want?" I asked. "If you have a message, give it at once."

"Don't hurry me," said he petulantly. "I want time to think. My message is worth a good price. A fine young fellow like you wouldn't cheat a poor man."

I would have loved to have opened the door and pitched him outside with his message, but my mother's look stopped me.

"We'll give you your due," she said. "You can trust me for that."

Suddenly he became humble again.

"Yes, ma'am, I will trust you."

He fumbled in his rags and took out several things before he found what he wanted. He looked at these secretly before putting them back, but at last he opened his hand to show the token he had.

It was a small sharp-bladed knife with a horn handle in which were carved the initials, "J.F.".

My mother's face became as white as the wall. I knew that knife well, for I had last seen it in the hands of my father. And although he had never known my father, Billy guessed whose knife it was.

"Jim Farrell," he said softly. "That's his knife."

He leaned forward to take it. The beggar put it swiftly behind his back and snarled:

"Hands off! What about my price?"

"The message," said my mother faintly.

"You'll have your price," I said angrily. "Give your message."

"You're three against one, three against one," said the old mountebank maddeningly. "It's a hard, wicked world for a poor man."

"What is your price?" asked Billy, in despair at ever hearing the message.

Mikus gave a cunning look around the room.

"First I'll have that knife you've been using on the harness. A knife for a knife is fair."

Billy silently handed him the knife, and Mikus laid my father's knife on the table.

"Then I must have two paper pounds—no, five, I meant——"

"Very well," said I. "When you've told us what you have to say, you'll get five pounds."

I hoped we had five pounds in the house. It was a huge sum of money to us.

Mikus sent his eye round the room again, but Billy said:

"And that is all you'll get. Out with it now, or else be off with you!"

They measured each other. Then Mikus dropped his eyes. He seemed to sense that he could push us no further. He said:

"Very well. But you'd be long sorry if you didn't get my message. It's all very queer and I don't rightly understand it. It could be that you're up to no good yourselves."

"Never mind that," said Billy.

"There's no need to be so touchy," said Mikus, who was beginning to recover his perkiness. "I've come a long way out of my way to find you. I usually stay more to the north, in Donegal mostly, where the country is hilly and sweet, and the people are poor and kindly. But a while ago, for a certain reason, I travelled south to the County of Mayo, and I followed the coast road all the way. Have you ever been there, young fellow?"

"No," said I, trying to humour him, "though I hear it's a fine place."

" 'Tis all that. There's huge purple mountains rising straight out of the sea, and heathery bogs stretching away as far as the eye can travel. The big road goes inland a piece, but by the coast there is a little road, and that was the way that I went. I passed by the islands and the landing-places where the islandmen bring in their boats, and I came beyond the villages to the loneliest road in all Ireland. And there one morning I found a young man lying on the roadside.

"Oh, he was a pretty young man, with strong black hair and a skin like a girl's. But he was dying. I gave him water from a spring that was there, and he thanked me and lay so still. Then he began to repeat a name, 'Jim Farrell, Jim Farrell', over and over. I thought this was his own name, and I said:

" 'Where do you come from, Jim?'

"He shook his head and pointed to the sea.

" 'I came from out there—a message from Jim Farrell.'

"He was silent so long that I thought he was gone. Then he began again: 'Jim Farrell, Jim Farrell.' "

" 'Give me the message,' I said. 'I'll give the message.'

"Then he started to ramble about a place where he lived when he was a boy. There was a lot about boats, and his mother, and he seemed to be arguing with someone. Then he remembered the message, and suddenly he clutched my arm and squeezed till his fingers left marks on my skin. He told me to come to this place.

" 'Find Mrs. Farrell at once, at once! Tell her Jim is alive and the boy must go and find him. He has found it—we both found it. Tell her that—tell her that!'

" 'I'll tell her that,' said I. 'What did you find?'

"But he wouldn't say. He began to rave again. Then suddenly he got quiet and he said:

" 'Look in my pocket—Jim's knife—show it to her.'

"That was the last thing he said. I found the knife, and then I set out to find Mrs. Farrell. That was a harder task than I thought it would be. Before I left that place I went

along the shore looking for the wreckage of a boat, but I only found a few spars and an old water-barrel, empty. They could have belonged to anyone. Still, he said he came from the sea, so perhaps they were from his boat. There were bad storms this winter."

This was a very strange story to me. It filled my thoughts with wild speculations. I said:

"I knew my father is still alive."

My mother had followed Mikus's story eagerly, and now she took up the knife and stroked it softly. Billy said:

"What else did you take out of the young man's pockets besides the knife?"

Mikus stood up to his full height, the picture of insulted innocence.

"There's my thanks! There's all you can say! Accuse me of stealing—of robbing the dead—"

"Easy on, now," said Billy. "After all, if you had not taken charge of his property, anyone passing the road might have robbed him and we would have had no way of finding out who he was."

"That's right," said Mikus carefully, suspecting a trap.

"So it was just as well you took his things," resumed Billy, "for now you can show them to me, and I can describe them to his people. For I think I know who your pretty young man was, peace to his soul."

"Amen," said Mikus uneasily.

He turned his back on us and fumbled in his rags again. When he turned around, he had a number of small objects displayed in each grimy palm. There was a folding knife, a screwdriver, a carpenter's rule and one or two small tools of the sort you might expect to find in the pockets of a man who was useful with his hands. There was a rabbit's tail, too, which the country people sometimes carried for luck. It had not brought much luck to its last owner. All the tools had rusty spots, as if they had been in the water.

I got a pain in my heart for the young man who had carried them, and whose boat must have gone down in the dark of the storm within sight of land.

Billy took each of the things in turn and examined it carefully before laying it on the table.

"I'm afraid they're all a rather common type," he said with a sigh. "Still, someone might recognize them. Another pound for the lot," he said to Mikus.

"Done!" said Mikus. "I can be generous sometimes."

I think I never saw a more ridiculous sight than his expression of aristocratic philanthropy at that moment. It was quite a shock when he discarded it and we saw again the more credible cunningness in his eye.

"And I'd like my money now, sir. I'm a poor man, and I must look out for myself."

My mother, who had not spoken a word all this time, got up now and went to the corner press. She took out a tin box and brought it to the table, when she counted out six pound notes. She handed these to Mikus, whose little weaselly eyes had followed every movement.

"This is every penny I have," she said, "but you're more than welcome to it, for the sake of the news you have brought me."

Mikus took the money, and peered into the now empty box. His look said quite plainly that if there had been more he would have demanded it. My mother, poor simple woman, misunderstood his look.

"You need not be slow to take the money," she said. "You have been very generous in coming so far out of the way to find me. I wish we could do more for you. Billy! Perhaps there would be some work he could do on the farm."

She turned back to Mikus.

"You're lucky that it's springtime, for that is the busiest time with us. I'm sure you could help us in many ways.

And it would be better for you not to be roaming the country alone."

Billy and I looked at each other. The beggarman's face was a study. He coughed delicately.

"It's this way, ma'am," he said. "I have the cough, do you understand, and any exertion is bad for me. There's no one likes an honest day's work more than myself, but for reasons of health, ma'am, I must decline your kind offer."

"Oh, I'm sorry," said my mother. "Of course your health comes first, though we would have been glad of your help. But at least you'll spend the night with us, or longer if you wish."

Billy and I looked at each other again, but this time in consternation. For there was Mikus with his thumbs in the tattered armholes of his waistcoat, swinging triumphantly from heel to toe, with his chest stuck out. He avoided our eyes, and addressed himself carefully to my mother.

"It would be churlish of me, ma'am, to refuse such a kind invitation. So I'll say, thank you kindly, I'll be glad to stay. 'Tis a treacherous time of the year, and bad for the weakness on the chest. I'll be safer on the road when the weather gets warmer."

And the old rascal sat down comfortably in Billy's chair by the fire.

I did not know what to do. I would not for the world have opposed my mother to-night, and still I certainly did not want Mikus as an old man of the sea until the summer. He looked a proper old thief and rogue, and I knew neither Billy nor I would ever have a moment's peace as long as he was about the place. But just now there was nothing more to be said. My mother began to unfold the settle bed by the fire.

"You won't mind sleeping in the kitchen," she said. "Our house is small, and we have little enough to offer to strangers."

Mikus raised a majestic forefinger.

"If you'll believe me, ma'am, I prefer to sleep in the kitchen. It's warmer, and the crickets keep me company."

While my mother made up the bed, Mikus discoursed on the meanness of people.

"They'd give more to an old dog than they'd give to one of God's poor," said he piously, "but of course I don't complain. I simply put a curse on them, the poor man's curse, and I go away like a Christian, knowing that I'll have the laugh on them on the Day of Judgment."

"You couldn't do fairer than that," said Billy.

"Now, I know many a man who would not have bothered to deliver that message. They'd have forgotten, or they'd have thought there would be something in it for themselves. But I said to myself, 'Mikus,' I said, 'go and find this poor woman and give her the message from her husband, and who knows but she may be guided to reward you. And maybe she'll do more for you when her husband comes home with his fortune made.' "

"That's another story," said I.

"Ah, you're hard-hearted," said Mikus. "The young are often hard-hearted. That's the way of the world."

And for all his tone of pious resignation, he gave me a look of intense dislike, which I returned with interest.

The hour was late now, and my mother distributed the brochan, a kind of thin, sweet porridge that we always had for supper. Mikus drained a huge mugful of it, and then hinted that it was time we quitted his bedroom and left him to sleep. He stretched his long arms upwards in a yawn, looking like an old wintry tree. Then he said:

"I nearly forgot to tell you one more thing that the young man said. I forgot because I don't know what he meant. It sounded like the name of a place, an island, perhaps, by the sound of it."

"An island," my mother whispered, "yes, an island. What was its name?"

"Inishmanann," said Mikus. "He said it several times, and I'm sure that was it. Inishmanann. I never heard of an island of that name."

"Perhaps he was raving," said Billy quickly.

"Maybe," said Mikus.

We wished him good night, and went to our rooms. Billy and my mother had the two rooms off the kitchen, and I climbed up to the loft, where I had a stretcher-bed among the harness. I liked it up there in the quiet, with the sweet leathery smell all about me. It had been an exciting day, from my meeting with Joe and his strange collection of animals, to the arrival of Mikus with his story. And I had a strong sense that this was only the beginning. I lay there in the dark for a long time, turning it all over in my mind, and fell asleep at last full of wild plans and hopes.

⭑ III ⭑

Billy was about first in the morning, as usual. He came to the foot of my ladder and called:

"Michael! Come down till you see what's happened!"

I tumbled out of bed and pulled on my clothes. I came down the ladder rubbing the sleep out of my eyes, and paused in astonishment at what I saw.

There was no sign of Mikus. The settle bed was empty, and the blankets were gone too. The corner press where my poor innocent mother had gone for the money was ransacked and its contents strewn on the floor. She had spoken the truth when she said she had no more money in the house, but the old scoundrel had not believed her. Then he had scattered everything about in a rage, it seemed, and had finally gone off with the blankets, for they were the most valuable things in the kitchen.

"I found the back door swinging open when I came out of my room," said Billy. "I must have slept like a log, for I heard no sound during the night."

"Poor fellow," said I, in mock sympathy. "The night air will have injured his delicate chest!"

Billy wished the night air good hunting.

Hearing our voices, my mother came out of her room. She understood what had happened at once.

"The poor man," she said. "I should not have left him with such temptation."

She dropped on her knees before the press, and began to put back her scattered things.

"Perhaps it's just as well this happened," said Billy in a low voice to me. "We're not likely to see the bold Mikus in these parts for a while. Last night I thought he was going to settle down here for life."

As it was Sunday, we had to hurry about our work so as to be in time to go to Church. I went to the milking, and Billy to the shed where he sorted potato seed for the next day's planting. There was a special kind of potato that did well with us, and Billy tended the crop like a hen with her chickens. He never forgot his self-imposed task of teaching me, and he would call me to see how he cut the seed, and how a special turn of the knife got the best results. He had taught me how to plough too, though I despaired of ever being as good a ploughman as himself. He had a way of hitching the reins around his head so that his two hands were free to guide the plough. The slightest turn of his head then kept the mare on her course. I tried it once when I was alone, and the result was lamentable. I will not soon forget Billy's expression as he stood surveying my crooked drills.

"Very nice, Michael; very nice," said he solemnly. "It's a new plan to fool the wire-worm, I suppose."

On Sunday afternoons my mother always put on her best things and came out with Billy and me to "walk the land", as the saying is. We went to each of our little fields in turn, noting with joy how the crops were beginning to push their way above the ground. We visited the cows, who were out enjoying the fresh spring grass, and the fat, clever pigs that, for all their cleverness, would make fine bacon for next winter.

My mother never said a word about the strange message she had got last night, and though I was burning with curiosity I was slow to open the subject. Billy said nothing about it either, though he fell into such long silences from time to time that I judged he was thinking it all over.

It was not until after our evening meal, when we were sitting by the fire again, that Billy took his pipe out of his mouth and said:

"I think, ma'am, the time has come to tell the boy the whole story."

"Yes, I must tell it," said my mother. "I suppose I knew I must tell it some day."

My heart thumped with excitement now that I was on the edge of having the mystery solved. I could see that Billy knew all about it, though he listened very attentively, leaning back in his chair with his eyes closed.

"When we first came to live here," my mother began, "we found the farm in very bad condition. The last owners had been careless, and they had let the hedges grow until they overshadowed half the fields. The fields were boggy for want of proper drainage, and the soil was poor, because crop after crop had been taken off it without manuring it in between. The house was just as bad. The thatch leaked, the floors were uneven and the walls had not been painted for years. It stood with its toes in a sea of mud, in which the cattle sank up to the knees."

I could not imagine our trim farm in this state. Now there was no better land in the county, and our house was as neat as anyone could imagine. The farmyard was cobbled, the thatch was a rich golden-brown—altogether it was the envy of the whole neighbourhood.

"It's hard to imagine it now," said my mother, looking with pleasure round her warm, cosy kitchen. "We had to work very hard for the first few years. Jim—your father—was a good farmer, and gradually he got the place into proper condition. He cut the hedges and drained the fields. He built the byre and the hayshed and he put a new roof on the stables. He cobbled the yard and mended the thatch, and at last he had it all exactly right.

"But this did not satisfy him. After years of toil, it was not enough to have ordinary farm work to do. He made some furniture for the house, and that kept him occupied for a while. But then he got restless again, and he took to going into the town as often as he had time. When he would come back he would tell me that he had been down to the docks looking at the boats, and that it would be a good thing for us to own a boat of our own, for lobster fishing.

" 'A pookawn would be just right,' he would say. 'There isn't enough work for me on the farm as long as we have Jamesey.' Jamesey Lynch was the man we had then. 'And there would be too much for me alone. So it would be an economy if I could go fishing sometimes and add to our income.'

"I said we had enough to live on, and needed no more. I implored him not to buy a boat, for I hate the sea. I don't trust it. One moment it's smiling at you and the next moment it takes your life. When I was a girl we lived by the sea. My father and my brother were lost at sea. I don't trust it.

"Your father agreed not to buy a boat for fishing, as I was so much against it, but still he kept going down to the docks, talking to the idle men that sit there on the walls all day, and listening to their silly stories.

"Oh, I'm not blaming him, indeed I'm not! He was always romantic, watching for adventures. He loved a story more than anything in the world.

"Then one day he came home on fire with a new idea."

"I remember that," I put in. "He was like a man that had found a crock of gold."

"He thought he had found one. He told me all about it, though I made him wait until you had gone to bed. I did not want your head to be filled with his kind of wild nonsense.

"That afternoon he had fallen into talk with an old man who was sitting on the quay wall trailing a fishing-line in the water. It was the old man's story that changed everything, that broke up our snug home, and sent your father off across the salt seas, chasing a rainbow.

"For the old man told him about Inishmanann, the lost island of Manannan, the old god of the sea. No one who went to the island had ever come back, the old man said, but according to the story, anyone who succeeded in returning would bring back something rare and valuable with him. I said it was wrong to believe these old pagan stories, that there never was a god of the sea called Manannan, and that he should be warned by the fact that no one who ever went to the island had come back. He said he knew all that, and still he kept returning to the subject of the island. He said there must be a real island of some sort, or else the story would not have lasted so long. There were people who said they had seen it, but they were afraid to land there. Perhaps they saw a mirage, but still he believed there was a real island.

"I asked him what he expected to find there.

" 'Not leprachauns and fairy gold,' he said, 'and still I'm sure there's something valuable there, whatever it is.'

" 'There's nothing there,' I said, 'and there is no island either.'

"But he would not believe that.

"Then one day he came home and told me he had bought a boat. My heart sank when I heard this.

" 'What kind of boat?' I asked.

" 'A fishing boat,' " he said, and he could not meet my eye. 'A black tarred pookawn. But I'm not going fishing. I'm going to find the lost island.' "

"I did not argue with him any more, for I could see

that he would never be happy until he had at least searched for his island. I asked him what he planned to do. He was so grateful to me for not opposing him any more that he told me all about it. It seemed that this was a particularly good boat, old and strong, and fit to brave the wildest Atlantic storms. I doubted that, but I said nothing. I did not really trust any boat, but I knew that the pookawns were well-built, and as seaworthy as any boat one is likely to find.

" 'The boat is at O'Neill's pier,' he said. 'We would like to call her Eileen, after you.'

"Even this could not make me like the idea.

" 'You say "we",' I said. 'Who is going with you?'

" 'Tomeen Connolly,' he said. 'He has wanted to go ever since he was a small boy, when his grand-uncle told him about Inishmanann. He's young and hardy, and a good sailor. It was Tomeen's grand-uncle that told me about the island too.'

" 'Then he has a lot to answer for,' I said.

" 'And I was thinking of taking Michael with us,' he finished.

"But I absolutely refused to allow this. You were only ten years old, and though you were as good as a man at some things, still I did not want to send everyone I had out on this wild-goose chase.

" 'If Michael goes, I go too,' I said, and I refused to budge from this.

"So he would not press me, for he knew how I hated the sea, and it was agreed that he and Tomeen would go alone."

I was boiling with questions by this time.

"Was Tomeen the 'pretty young man' that Mikus talked about?" I asked.

Billy took his pipe out of his mouth.

"I think so," he said. "Tomeen was a carpenter by

trade, and the things Mikus gave me looked as if they might have belonged to a carpenter."

"Yes, Tomeen was a carpenter," my mother went on, "and he was useful at fitting out the boat. All his brothers were wild ones. They left home very young, and scattered to all parts of the world. They were full of curiosity, that was the trouble with them. And the old man, their grand-uncle, was always sitting at home telling them strange wild tales about foreign places that he had never seen, until nothing would do them but to be off."

"I wonder what the 'something rare and valuable' is?" I said. "Perhaps the pirate O'Neill buried his treasure on the island——"

Billy burst out laughing.

"O'Neill didn't have any treasure that I ever heard," he said. "He was the queerest pirate in the world. He used to catch the smugglers on their way home from France, which was a great place for that sort of thing then, and he used to rob them and run in their stuff himself. They dared not complain, for they were breaking the law themselves. But he was caught at last, of course, as all criminals must be. No, I think O'Neill had no treasure, for all his loot was perishable."

"There were different stories about what was to be found," said my mother. "Some of them said the Tree of Knowledge grew there, and that if you ate some of its fruit you would know everything without going through the labour of studying. Then there was a story that there was some charm there that would turn everything it touched into gold. Oh, there were any number of old fairy-tales about it, that no one would believe, but no one doubted that there was an island—except myself. I never believed there was an island."

"And now Mikus says there is," I said softly.

"They got the boat ready," said my mother hurriedly,

"and at last, four years ago in May, they were ready to go. Jim had not told anyone where they were going, partly because he said voyages of this sort aroused too much interest, and partly because he did not want to be laughed at. The crops were well advanced, as the weather had been good that year, and he told Jamesey Lynch exactly what to do.

" 'We won't be gone for long,' he said to me. 'I'll be back before the hay is in.'

"They sailed away one lovely morning, very early. It had been a night of calm, but in the morning a breeze had come up.

" 'It's just come for us,' Jim said. 'We'll have weather like this all the time. I can feel it in my bones.'

"And so they had, for over a week. The sun shone every day, and there was the same soft gentle breeze, just strong enough for comfortable sailing. But after a week it changed. The skies blackened suddenly, and such a storm got up as I never hope to see again. The hay was battered down flat and the fields would have been waterlogged only for our fine new field drains. Everywhere I went I saw the pookawn before my eyes being tossed from wave to wave of the ocean, and going down at last into the stormy blackness.

"I went into the town to see old Bartley Connolly.

" 'Now look at what you've done', I said, 'with your stories and your fairy-tales. Oh, it's easy for you to sit here at home by the fire, while fine young men are swallowed up by the greedy sea. And if they don't come back, yours will be the blame!'

" 'They'll be all right,' he said, the old ruffian, as cool as a breeze. 'If they can't weather a little blow like that they're as well to be drowned, for they're no men.'

" 'You had no right to send them,' I said.

" 'I never sent them,' said he. 'I only told them the

stories when they asked me. I wouldn't go myself, I told them. It would be too dangerous for me. They may have thought I was daring them to go, but I was not. I can't help it if people are foolhardy.'

"There was truth in this, as I well knew. I myself had not been able to stop Jim from going.

"He saw by my face that I was no longer blaming him so much.

" 'And they had probably reached the island by the time the storm broke,' he said. 'They are likely enough sheltering there this moment.'

"It was no use staying any longer. I came away home and tried to take comfort from the old man's cheerfulness. And for a while I did hope they were safe. But as time went on and we heard no news of them I came to believe they must be drowned.

"I had other troubles too. Jamesey Lynch worked well enough as long as he thought Jim might be coming back. But by the end of the summer he seemed to have decided that he could do as he liked. You know the rest of the story, how he sold the stock and the corn and kept the money, until I had to get the police after him. And even then he got away with so much that we have been poor ever since. It all seems so long ago now."

I remembered this well. We had struggled along by ourselves, letting the land go to ruin, until the only thing left to do was to sell the farm. And then one day Billy came walking into the yard, and our troubles were over. He had even refused to take any wages until we had re-stocked the farm. I knew that we would never be able properly to repay him.

"That is the whole story," my mother went on, after a pause. "What to do next I do not know."

"I know what is to be done," said I. "I must follow my father's instructions. He said I was to go and find him."

"But can we believe Mikus?" said Billy. "He did not prove himself so trustworthy in other respects."

"I think he was telling the truth," I said. "He doesn't come from this part of the country, and how could he know the name of the island? And there is the knife."

"Yes, there is the knife," said my mother. "I'd know it anywhere."

"At least I can go into the town and find out more about this island."

"No one talks about the island except old Bartley Connolly," said my mother. "You must go to him. But listening to him, it all sounds like a story about giants and fairies. Perhaps if he thinks you are really going to go there, he may talk about it more seriously."

"And you can show him the things I got from Mikus," said Billy. "Perhaps he'll know for certain if they once belonged to Tomeen."

"Old Bartley never goes out now," said my mother. "You'll have to go to his own house to find him."

⋆ IV ⋆

So the next morning I drove off again to town, in the pony cart. It had rained all night, until daylight, and the road was covered with little pools. There was a great cleanness in the air, and the new leaves were intensely green. A young rabbit hopped by the roadside at one place, and then crouched in full view, pressing his furriness down into the wet grass. Mine was the only cart on the road, and the wheels and the pony's hooves made an empty faraway noise in the quiet. People came to their doors to watch me go by, and wondered, I suppose, why anyone would think of going to town on a Monday, when there was no market.

As we passed by the place where Mikus had lain two days ago, the pony bucked a little and tried to shy.

"Remember what Billy told you," I said to him.

He became quiet again, but his ears kept twitching nervously for a long time afterwards. I wondered where Mikus had gone. I hoped he had put a good distance between us, for I had no wish to see him again, although he had brought such good news.

When I reached the town I found it strangely quiet. It had always been market-day or fair-day when I was in town, and I missed the bustle and the clanking carts. I was surprised, too, to see the townspeople occupied in trading with each other. It would have surprised me less if I had found them all asleep, waiting for the country people to come in again. I felt awkward in my heavy clothes, for the first time in my life, and I left the main streets as soon as I could and drove down by back ways to the docks. This time I drove around by the big bridge and pulled up the pony at the door of Pete's cottage.

Mrs. Pete came out. Pete was gone fishing, she said, and would not be back till the evening. Joe had not gone, however, and she called him from the little back garden where he was planting cabbages.

We went into the kitchen, and I told them the story of the arrival of Mikus with the message and the knife. I told them the rest of the story of my father's adventures too, as I had heard it from my mother. Joe could hardly contain his excitement.

"We'll get a boat. We'll go at once. We'll get there in a week——"

"Don't you think it would be quicker to swim?" said Mrs. Pete sardonically. "And since you know exactly where to go——"

Joe grinned sheepishly.

"Well, anyway we won't waste any time," he said. "I'm coming with you, of course," he added to me.

"I had guessed that," said I. "But before we start thinking of boats we must visit old Bartley Connolly. He seems really to know something about the island."

Mrs. Pete knew where Bartley lived.

"He sits all day in the chimney-corner," she said, "waiting for a chance to tell his old stories to visitors. But hardly anyone will listen to him now. They think he is just a silly old man, and they laugh at him and tease him. But I remember him when he was younger, many years ago. He was not silly then. The house belongs to his grand-nephew, Roddy, who is a brother of Tomeen that went away with your father. His wife, Nora, looks after the old man."

"Will she let us in to see him?" I asked, while I tried to sort out this information.

"She won't want to let you in," said Mrs. Pete. "Not for yourselves, for she's a kindly creature, but she will not want to upset the old man. Tell her I sent you, and don't stay too long. Nora is a great friend of mine."

We left Mrs. Pete, promising to come back for dinner, and went across the footbridge over the dock. At the far side a row of thatched cottages stretched at right angles to the quay wall. There was a big green before them, on which geese were grazing. They stretched their necks and gave way to their queer, long, wavering cry. The Connollys lived in the second cottage. It was newly thatched and whitewashed, and a row of round stones on either side of the door had been whitewashed too.

A young woman came to the door in answer to our knock. She did not look too pleased at first when she heard we had come to visit Bartley, but when we told her that Mrs. Pete had sent us, she asked us to come in.

We stepped over the threshold into the kitchen.

"Here are two hardy lads to see you," said Nora, to an old man who was sitting on the hob, as close as he could to the small turf fire.

He was the oldest man I had ever seen, as old as a field, as the people say in our district. He was bent almost double over an ash stick which he had planted firmly between his feet. He wore a suit of homespun grey, darned in many places, and a battered black hat with a wide brim. He had a sparse white beard, and a little fringe of white hair showed under his hat at the back. His face was as withered as an old forgotten chestnut, and the same colour, and his shrewd grey eyes were all screwed up as he tried to examine us in the dimness.

"You're looking at my hat," he said at last, in a creaking voice. "I don't go out any more, and a man must wear a hat sometimes, so I wear mine in the house. It's a good hat."

"They want to hear some of your old yarns, Bartley," said Nora cheerfully.

She turned to us.

"Don't believe all you hear from him, or this place will get too small for you and you'll have to go roaming the world. He puts the poison into every young man that will listen to him. My Roddy won't listen, and I hope he never will."

"Sure, some of the people must stay at home," said Bartley, winking at us. "I never left home myself. I don't like danger and adventures. I only like talking about them."

"You like that, sure enough," said Nora.

She made us sit by the fire, and then she took down her shawl from the peg behind the door.

"I'm going into town for a message," she said. "Don't let the fire go out."

When she had gone, Bartley heaved a long wheezing sigh of relief.

"Women are useful," he said solemnly. "They can cook, some of them, and darn, and mind the children, but they don't like a man to be too independent. Now, Nora couldn't go into town without giving me a little job to keep me quiet."

He picked up the tongs and began to put the fire together.

"Do you know anything about Inishmanann?" I asked abruptly.

He paused with the tongs raised and looked at me sharply.

"You would be Jim Farrell's son. Have you heard from him?"

"Yesterday," I said, "for the first time in four years."

"And Tomeen?"

"Tomeen is dead."

I searched in my pockets and took out the carpenter's rule and the tools that Mikus had sold to Billy. I handed them to Bartley without a word, and I could see at once that he knew them.

"That's my old rule," he said in a trembling voice. "I lent it to Tomeen, and now it has come back."

He was silent all the time while I told the story. Then he said:

"Poor Tomeen. I well remember the morning he sailed away. The sun shone on the water and turned the boat into gold—a golden barque sailing the seas like in the high tales of long ago. When I saw that I said they would have luck. I said they would surely find the island and bring home the treasure that no man ever saw before."

"They must have found the island all right," said Joe. "And Tomeen told Mikus that they found the treasure too. We must go there at once."

"Yes, we must go there," I said to Bartley. "Maybe you can tell us what to do."

"Good!" said Bartley, giving a thump on the hearth with his stick so that the ashes flew up. "I'll tell you what I told your father.

"The stories say that Inishmanann was the last stronghold of Manannan, the old god of the sea. There is another island, called the Isle of Man, that belonged to him too, but there is no mystery about that place. People live there, and boats go in and out every day. But no one lives on Inishmanann, and no one seems to know exactly where it is. Sometimes it has happened that a boat was blown far out to sea, and the sailors said afterwards that they saw a high rocky island away to the north. But they never came close to it, and some of them doubted if it was a real island. They thought it might be Hy-Brazil, the fairy island that floats on the edge of the world, between the sea and the sky.

"I don't know how the story about the treasure began. There is an old story about a prince who went there once to ask for Manannan's help in battle, and perhaps it was he who told about the treasure."

"If I had my father safely home from the island, the treasure could stay there till the end of the world," said I.

"But of course, if we get there we'll have a look for it," said Joe. "A few doubloons and pieces of eight would buy a bigger boat for Pete."

"Another old story says that Manannan lives on the island still, and that if anyone lands there he makes them stay for ever. But if a person knew the right spells, he could make himself invisible to Manannan, and he could come away again in safety."

It was quite clear from the way the old man spoke that he more than half believed these stories. There were many like him, who spent the long winter evenings exchanging stories of fairies and witches, giants with three heads and eight legs, beautiful maidens and the King of Ireland's Son. They would sit in the dark kitchen with no light but the glow of the turf fire and the sudden little brilliance when they drew heavily on their pipes, and recall old tales they had heard from their grandfathers. I had often spent an evening in the company of the old story-tellers near our farm, and I saw that Bartley's yarns about the island followed their familiar pattern.

Suddenly the old man sat up and said:

"The queerest thing about Jim Farrell was that he told me he knew what the spells were that would make him invisible!"

I was staggered at this. I could not imagine my father making any such statement. I asked, seriously:

"Did he tell you what the spells are?"

Old Bartley shook his head.

"I asked him, but he wouldn't tell me. He laughed, and said: 'I think I know what those spells are, right enough.' "

An idea began to take shape in my mind. I asked:

"These men who say they saw Inishmanann, would you say they were good sailors?"

"They were safe enough in their own waters," said Bartley, "but they were no good if anything went wrong. Then the man who sailed for the island when I was a boy, he was a poor sailor, a dreaming sort of a man. Your father, now—he knew how to handle a boat. The fishermen about here had a great respect for him. They said he would have made a fortune out of the lobster-fishing if he had put his mind to it."

All this bore out my idea, but I said nothing about it to Bartley.

"What became of the dreamy man who tried to get to the island?" I asked.

" He was never seen again. One of the Spanish trawlers brought in a piece of his boat about a year afterwards, and it looked as if it had been a long time in the water."

The old man looked worriedly at us.

"The more I remember the misfortunes that fell on everyone that tried to reach that island, the more I think the two of you would be better to stay at home."

"But the treasure—" said Joe.

"And my father," said I. "We must go."

"Well, I don't like it," said Bartley. "When grown men can't get there, how could two young lads like you do it?"

"We might bring Pete," said Joe.

"And what about Mrs. Pete?" asked Bartley. "Will you leave her alone at home? How much do you know about boats?" he asked me.

"Nothing," I confessed, "but I suppose I could learn."

"It takes years to learn about boats. Leave it alone—

drop the whole idea. You'll only be lost like all the others."

I stood up to go.

"We'll think about it anyway. That won't do any harm."

He looked at me eagerly. His wrinkled old face was full of excitement. Suddenly I realized that he was really urging us to go, and hoping that his protests would have the effect of spurring us on. Just as we reached the door I said:

"I nearly forgot to ask you the most important thing—how we are to get to the island? Must we search the whole North Atlantic for it?"

Bartley chuckled creakily to himself.

"Oh, I can give you very precise directions."

"Directions!" I exclaimed. "I had no idea there were directions for getting there."

"When that Prince sailed for Inishmanann long ago," said Bartley solemnly, "he went to a sage of his acquaintance to ask him how to get there—just as you have come to me. He was told to set the stern of his boat against the Eagle's Rock when the tide was full, and to sail north of south and south of north for seven days and seven nights, and then he would reach the island. But his boat was called the *Wave-Rider*, a long slim boat like a lance." The old man laughed and rubbed his hands. "An old tarry pookawn would hardly keep a boat like that in sight for half a day."

We thanked him and stepped outside into the sunshine.

"He's a very aggravating old man," said Joe. "He makes me want to get to that island if it costs me my life."

"That's exactly how he got all the young lads he knew to go off in search of adventures," I said. "We'll get to that island all right."

"But we must make ourselves invisible," said Joe seriously.

I looked at him in astonishment, and then burst out laughing before I could stop myself.

"Surely you don't believe that part of the story?"

"Well," said Joe uneasily, "I don't know that it isn't true. I'm sure the animals can talk on Saint John's Eve, anyway."

I did not know what to say. It was obviously no use arguing with Joe about it, so I went on:

"I think that what my father guessed was that there was difficulty in landing on the island. People say it's high and rocky, and there may be strong currents and high seas around it. It seems to me that the people who went there were shipwrecked. Manannan got them then, without a doubt."

Joe looked a little shamefaced.

"Yes. That's a more reasonable idea," he said, with a grin. "I don't much like the thought of being invisible."

"Then there is the question of how to get there," I said. "south of north and north of south."

"That's a straight line," said Joe. "We can simply take a bearing from the Eagle's Rock."

This explanation was so simple that it seemed like the truth. The Eagle's Rock was a tall narrow peak that stuck up out of the water just beyond O'Neill's pier. The highest tide never covered it, and it carried a red light on its tip at night.

"I have a map over in my place," said Joe. "Let's go and look at it."

Tacked on to the wall above the rat's cage was an old yellowed map of the harbour. It showed the docks and the river estuary, and the islets and lighthouses close by. The Eagle's Rock was marked, with a little lantern drawn to show that it carried a light.

"If we take a bearing from the Rock out through the mouth of the bay, we'll sail half a mile south of the Fort Island," said Joe, drawing his finger across the map to show this.

The Fort Island was the biggest of the three that lay across the mouth of the bay.

"I hear it gets pretty rough outside the islands," I said.

"I've been out there with Pete," said Joe. "It's bad in winter, all right. I've heard them say that in winter sometimes the waves rise so high that they hide the highest point of the island from a man in a boat."

We were silent for a moment, thinking of this, and then I said, trying to sound cheerful:

"That was in winter, of course. We probably won't meet anything like that."

Joe drew his fingers on across the map till it ran over the edge.

"Where is the lost island?" he said. "That's the problem. It could be thousands of miles away."

"Seven days and seven nights is not long," I said. "And I'm sure the difficulty is not one of distance. After all, men have sailed the Atlantic in small boats before."

"Perhaps the island itself becomes invisible," said Joe, and then he looked embarrassed.

But suddenly another idea had struck me.

"Perhaps it does," I said excitedly. "Perhaps that's exactly what happens!"

Joe looked at me in astonishment.

"I thought you didn't believe that sort of thing," he said.

"There are more ways than one for it to become invisible," I said. "Perhaps there's a lot of fog there!"

"And that would explain its looking like Hy-Brazil," said Joe, " 'floating between the sea and the sky'."

"We'll soon find out when we get there," said I. "Now all we have to do is to get a boat."

⋆ V ⋆

"A boat!" said Joe. "That won't be so easy. If only Pete would come with us!"

"Do you think he would?" I asked. "I don't think he'll like the idea of our going alone. And neither will my mother."

We sat there gloomily, wishing we were at least five years older. Joe lifted his rat out of its cage and stroked it gently, while the tip of its tail twitched a little. I moved away, but he was too preoccupied to notice. We both felt quite well able to set out for the lost island together, but unless we slipped away without telling anyone, this would be out of the question. For many reasons this was impossible. We could not hope to equip and victual a boat without attracting attention, and anyway we had no boat to start with.

"We had better tell Pete all about it," said Joe at last. "He may have an idea about what to do."

He put the rat back and closed the cage, and we came out on to the quay. The sun had almost dried up the ground, and there was a soft steaminess in the air. We looked out beyond the pier wall, to where little white-capped choppy waves were dancing in the sun outside.

Suddenly Joe pointed.

"Look! That's Pete's boat coming in!"

A black sail was moving quickly towards the mouth of the dock.

"How do you know that's Pete's boat?"

"I'd know that patch on the sail anywhere," said Joe. "I wonder why he's coming home so early—he usually spends the whole day at sea. Come along—we'll go to meet him."

Already he was running towards the footbridge over the lock. I followed, and we reached the place where Pete always tied up, just as the pookawn tacked into the little dock. The water below us was as smooth as oil, though a little swell sent it washing up and down against the wall every minute or two.

Joe was watching the hooker's approach with his hands on his bent knees and his neck craned forward. He looked uneasy.

"I don't see Pete," he said. "Jerry Fahy is doing it all himself."

I could see a red-haired man of about Pete's age standing at the helm. He saw us too, but he made no sign, except that he dropped his eyes as he ran the boat in alongside the quay wall. Joe caught the rope he threw and wound it round one of the squat stone bollards. Then he called out:

"Hi, Jerry! Where's Pete?"

Mrs. Pete came out of the house just then, and stood for a moment at the doorway before moving slowly towards us. Jerry glanced unhappily at her as he said:

"Pete is below. He got hurt when he fell down the ladder, and I came home. I thought that was the best thing to do."

"It was, to be sure," said Joe.

He took a flying leap on to the deck, and hurried down into the hold. A moment later his head popped up again.

"He's not too bad," he called out to Mrs. Pete. "He's hurt his leg, I think."

While Mrs. Pete and Joe were calling the neighbours

and having Pete brought into the house and sending for the doctor, I spent the time usefully in consoling Jerry Fahy. He was sitting in the boat with his red head in his hands, blaming himself for the accident. I chatted with him of other things until the doctor arrived. Then Jerry said:

"Go up and find out what the doctor says, like a good boy, for I can't bear to go myself."

In a few minutes I was back to tell him that Pete had broken his leg, and would be in bed for a few weeks. But it would be months before he would be able to handle a boat again.

"And can't I go fishing for him until he's all right again?" said Jerry.

I stayed with him until Joe came out of the house with bread and butter sandwiches in his hands.

"No dinner to-day," he said, handing me some. "I told Mrs. Pete we wouldn't starve for once."

Jerry went home then, and we sat there on the deck munching, in the sun.

"This means Pete won't be able to come with us," said Joe. "In fact, it makes me wonder whether I'll be able to go at all."

"Jerry Fahy said he'll go fishing for Pete," I said.

"So he will—he has no boat of his own. Then the best thing to do is to tell Pete all about it, and ask his advice."

I liked this idea, for Pete was a good sailor, and level-headed. However, I was quite certain I would set out for that island as soon as possible, even if I had to go alone.

"A boat, a boat," said Joe. "A boat is what we need. We can't take Pete's boat, because Jerry will want it for the fishing."

"Would someone lend us a boat?"

"The fishing-boats are too valuable to lend," said Joe. "They are the whole livelihood of the people here. And we would have to explain too many things."

"It would cost a lot to buy one," I said. "All my mother can give will be wanted for food and equipment."

A hungry-looking seagull landed on the gunwale and snapped his strong yellow beak. Joe handed him the last of his bread. Immediately a squalling flock began to wheel all around us. I threw them a small piece of my bread, which was all that remained, and they scrambled and fought madly for it.

"Come along, before they knock us into the water," I said.

We climbed ashore and ran down the pier, past the houses, to where a long slip was built out into the dock, against the high wall that kept out the winds from the bay. A narrow canal ran from the dock basin across the pier, through a high double gate and into a big square yard. The gates stood open and on them was painted "P. Conway, Boat-Building and Repairs". The canal was crossed by a narrow wooden bridge, and beyond was the open water of the bay.

"That's Pat Conway's boatyard," said Joe. "He floats the boats in and out on the canal."

He showed me the miniature lock gates at the mouth of the canal.

"Pat let me work the gate once," he said, "but you never know what humour he'll be in, so it's best to keep away from him. The canal is just wide enough to let a pookawn go through."

We peeped in through the open gates. There were several boats there, up on blocks, in different stages of repair. Most of them were pleasure boats, with long white clean lines to them, but there were one or two hookers as well. One of these was having its rudder repaired, and another had a new white plank in its side.

"Some of the men mend their own boats," said Joe.

"Not that they need much mending, if they're well handled."

There was no one near the gate, and without saying a word, we slipped inside. How tall the boats looked out of the water! We walked all round the nearest ones and I was amazed to find that there was as much below as above water when the boat was afloat.

"It would be dangerous in high seas otherwise," said Joe. "Now here's one," he stretched up his hand and patted the hull of a big two-masted yacht. "There would be a fine boat to go treasure-hunting in. A ketch is easy to handle too."

"What's a ketch?" I asked.

"*That's* a ketch," said Joe simply, slapping the hull.

I looked at it with the respect one gives to new knowledge.

"One could sail the Atlantic in that boat," said Joe. "I wish we could have it to sail to our treasure island."

"I'm afraid we'll have to be content with something plainer than that," said I.

Suddenly a man appeared from the other side of the ketch. He must have moved very lightly, for neither of us had heard his approach. He was short, and his stomach stuck out in front in a blue fisherman's jersey. He had one of those fat, round, smiling faces that always make one distrust the owner, for the hearty laugh has something wary in it, and the little eyes dart watchfully about like a snake looking for a place to strike. He was smiling affably now, but his eyes were cold.

"Well, gentlemen! Thinking of buying a boat, ha-ha!"

Joe shifted uneasily.

"Hello, Mr. Conway," he said.

Mr. Conway said:

"And who is your young friend? And why are you hang-

ing about amusing yourself instead of being at home looking after Pete?"

All this was said with the same smile. Joe flushed.

"Pete is well looked after," he said. "We just came in to look at the boats. Michael, here, is thinking of buying one."

I started.

"I wish I had the money to buy one," I said.

I looked at Joe. I didn't like his telling Pat Conway that we were interested in boats. I could see that he was a bit annoyed with himself for having done so.

I expected Pat to burst out laughing, but he did not. He glanced quickly from one to the other of us, with his eyes half shut. Then he became once more open and friendly and anxious to please. But both of us had seen that look, and we heartily wished ourselves outside his gate again.

"If you're looking for a boat, Pat Conway is your man," he said, gripping us each by the elbow and holding us one on either side of him. "Don't mind that old ketch—that's a fancy job. Come along with me and I'll show you something fit for heavy work."

And he marched us quickly up the yard away from the gates.

I did not like this development. I noticed uneasily that a little fox of a man with cross eyes had slipped from behind another boat that he had been painting, and was engaged in closing the double gates on to the quay. Pat saw me looking back and began to talk faster.

"I know the very thing—a sharp stern to run before the wind, not too much sail, a little weather helm and you could sail to Timbuctoo—there she is!"

There she was, sure enough, a competent-looking little ship, about thirty feet long, with a little cabin. She badly needed paint, but even to my eye she looked a sensible boat with no nonsense about her. Joe's eyes lit up when he saw her.

"The very thing!" he said, and stopped.

"The very thing for what?" asked Pat, and he wasn't smiling now. "Inside here, please, and tell me what's the game!"

He shoved us into a kind of little office built against the back wall of the yard. It was furnished with a table and a chair. Some coils of rope lay in one corner. The rest of the space was taken up with heaps of papers of all descriptions, mostly old bills and receipts, I thought. They looked like the accumulation of years.

Pat locked the door and put his back to it. He stood there a moment staring at us, as if he wished to read our minds. Suddenly he barked:

"Who sent you? Out with it!"

Joe looked desperately about for a way of escape.

"No one sent us," I said.

"Come, now, I heard you talking there by the ketch. What's all this about a treasure island?"

Neither of us said a word.

"You were up this morning with old Bartley Connolly," said Pat. "You told him you know about an island with buried treasure on it."

"How do you know that?" I asked quickly.

"There isn't much I don't know," said Pat with a leer. "Bartley told the next man that came in. Bartley is a very old man, remember. And the news of Tomeen Connolly's death could not go unnoticed."

I resolved there and then that I would practise holding my tongue, so that I would be able to do so when I would be old. Still it seemed that Bartley had not told the whole story.

"I'll make a bargain with you," said Pat. "You'll tell me what information you have, and I'll fit out a boat for you to go after the treasure. You'll find it and bring it home and then we'll go an even halves."

This was a very tempting offer. I could not see how we were going to get a boat by any ordinary means. But I did not want to tell Pat that the search for the treasure was the smallest part of our business, and that it seemed very doubtful that there was any treasure to be found at all. I had come to the conclusion that the "treasure" was something that would not appeal to Pat—contentment with one's lot, perhaps, arising out of thankfulness at a safe return home!

"All I can tell you is that we heard of an island, and they say that whoever gets there will find treasure," I said.

"Where is the island?"

I would not say, for of course I did not know. Pat stormed and raged, and threatened to cut us up in pieces so small that no one would be able to put us together again. Joe's eyes got bigger and bigger as he listened, but he said nothing. I knew that Pat would not dare to injure us, at least for the moment, so I let him rip ahead until he had used up all the language he knew.

Then he started on a new tack. We were good lads, clever lads, out to make our way in the world. Pat was the man for us. Pat knew every trick worth knowing. If we followed his advice we would be millionaires in a few years.

"If we're not in gaol," I said to myself.

Pat was full of goodwill towards everyone, especially towards the widow and the orphan. He knew everything that had happened in the town for the last hundred years.

"There was O'Neill, now, the man they call the pirate. As decent a man as ever grew hair. He made his fortune in this very place."

"But wasn't he caught and put in gaol in the end, and his boat burned?" said Joe.

Pat sighed heavily.

"He was unlucky," he said. "There's no need for a person to have such bad luck. Now, that boat I showed you out in the yard is the twin brother of O'Neill's boat, built at the same time, as fast as O'Neill's boat and faster. Wouldn't it be a fine thing to go treasure-hunting in a pirate's boat, eh?"

My heart raced at the prospect. It was not my business to judge O'Neill. Times were hard when he did his smuggling, and the people thought the taxes were unjust. And whether he was good or bad, he must surely have been a pleasanter character than Pat Conway.

There was no time to make up my mind. I tried to look Pat in the eye as I said:

"We can't tell you any more about the island and the treasure, but if you give us a boat we'll give you half of whatever we bring home. Of course we may not find any treasure at all."

Pat stared at us sourly for a long time. I guessed at what he was thinking, that no one would set out on a voyage without knowing where he was going, and that we must surely have more information than we had given him. At last he said:

"That doesn't sound a very good bargain for me. I might never see you again."

"True enough," said I, more cheerfully than I felt. "We might be drowned."

"And then I'd never see my good boat again either. I can see that the best thing for me would be to send one of my own men with you. Would you agree to that?"

Here was something that needed thinking out. It looked as if we would have to go alone unless we accepted this offer. Billy was no sailor, and besides, if he came with us my mother would be at home alone. Pat's man would probably be an experienced sailor, on the other hand, and would make up for my drawbacks in that respect. But then

Pat was quite capable of instructing his man to knock us into the sea and sail home alone as soon as we had found the treasure. I decided that we would have to deal with this possibility when the time would come.

"That would be a good plan," I said. "We would need three to manage the boat, I suppose. As for the treasure, if we find any you're welcome to half of it. Do you agree, Joe?"

"Yes," said Joe. "And what's more, we'll stick to our bargain."

"So will I, young fellow," said Pat heartily, so heartily that my heart sank.

I would rather have gone into partnership with Joe's rat than with Pat Conway. Still, there was no alternative, and we must only learn to be always on the watch for treachery.

Pat opened the door casually, trying to look as if he had never held it threateningly shut against us.

"We'll go and find the new member of your crew," he said, stepping out into the sunshine.

We followed with a great sense of relief in our freedom. Pat walked down the yard a little ahead of us. I noticed that the gates were open again.

The foxy man was back at his painting, but he was not able to look as affable as Pat. He gave us a quick sideways look as we approached, and his efforts at a smile were comical. It was like the smile of the fox the moment before he grabs the duck. Pat called out heartily:

"Come over here, Matt, and meet your new shipmates!"

Matt put down his brush and began to sidle towards us. My heart sank even lower when I saw that he was not even able to walk straight—he walked like a man who is always either aiming or expecting a blow. Pat whispered:

"That's Matt Raftery. He's a fine sailor, and he knows

the waters around here like the back of his hand. You'll be in good hands, you may be sure."

And he gave us a satisfied smile, with all his teeth showing.

Matt stood before us, looking us up and down, and it was plain that he did not like what he saw.

"Well, Matt, how would you like to go treasure-hunting with these brave young lads?" said Pat.

"That one is a bit on the small side," said Matt, pointing a claw-like finger at Joe.

He sounded like a woman in the market buying chickens.

"Good goods in small parcels," said Pat loudly, slapping Joe on the shoulder. "Eh, my lad?"

"That's right," said Joe, trying to edge away.

But Pat held him in a tight grip.

"With Matt for skipper, there won't be much you won't know about boats by the time you come home. Matt knows how to teach young lads, don't you, Matt?"

Matt leered in a satisfied way.

"That I do," he said.

He spat on his hands and rubbed them together, and was about to explain his methods of teaching young lads when Pat said hastily:

"You'll get a free education from Matt."

He glared at Matt, and his look plainly ordered him to hold his tongue. I could see that unless we were ready at the right time, our chances of coming back from our voyage alive would be small. But this was not the time to speak my mind, and when I looked at Joe I could see that he too had decided to say nothing.

Matt shuffled back to his painting again, and as he picked up his brush he began to sing an evil little song to himself. It was a song about pirates, that I had often heard sung in fun. But it did not sound at all funny as Matt sang it.

Pat hurried us out of earshot and said to Joe:

"You can tell Pete that everything will be all right. Matt will look after you well and bring you home safely. I'd go myself only I can't leave the yard, but I'm doing the best I can in sending my man instead."

He made it sound as if his only interest was in doing us a kindness.

"Now all you have to do is to tell me all you know about this island——"

"We know enough to set our course," I said, "but we won't tell until we're ready to go."

"Fair enough—you must protect yourself," said Pat heartily. "How do you know you can trust me?"

I avoided his eye and said again:

"I'll tell you when we're ready to go."

"Well now, we must get on with the business of fixing up the boat," said Pat. "It will take time, and I haven't any men to spare, especially with Matt going away. So the two of you had better come in here every day and do a bit of work on your boat yourselves. You'll get to know her that way."

I was delighted at this idea. I was so much afire now with the idea of setting out that I would have begun work there and then, if that had been possible. I tried to disguise my eagerness, and simply agreed that it sounded a good plan. Joe said that Pete would have to be consulted before we finally would agree to go. But of course it would be many days before Pete would be well enough to be asked questions and worried about our problems.

"You can start to fit out the boat anyway," said Pat, "and if Pete doesn't approve there will be no harm done."

By this suggestion he betrayed his eagerness. We left him then, hardly knowing whether to be pleased or not about our day's work.

★ VI ★

We walked up the pier to Pete's house without saying a word. It was well on in the afternoon now, and high time for me to be moving home. My pony was knocking the stones with one hoof, impatient to be gone, and he had mowed down the grass of the green all around him, as far as he could reach.

Joe brought him some bread out of the house, and as he fed him with it he said quietly:

"I won't worry Pete with talk of the boat until everything is ready. Then he can tell me if he doesn't want me to go."

I wondered if my mother and Billy would agree that I should accept Pat's offer. I shivered a little with excitement as I thought of the adventures and dangers that might be ahead. I had no idea what these would be—sea-serpents and sharks, perhaps, and storms, certainly. I was impatient to start the work.

"I'll come into town early to-morrow," I said, "and we'll go to Pat Conway's yard together."

"I hope he won't have changed his mind by then," said Joe anxiously.

"I'm quite certain he won't," I said. "If there is anything to be dug up, Pat Conway is going to make sure that he gets his share of it, and more."

I climbed into the cart and took the reins, while Joe undid the rope that tied the bridle to an iron post put there for the purpose. When he felt himself free, the pony shook his head till his mane flew about him. Then he gave a long wild whinny and set off at a hand-gallop towards the town. I stood up in the cart and shouted to him while we bounced along, for I always loved this wild streak in him. I looked back once, and there was Joe still standing there, waving to me.

We got home at a smart trot, for the pony seemed to feel the excitement of action in the air. I wanted to shout to him again and again, for I felt I was on the edge of something marvellous, something that would make the whole world look different ever after.

When I drove into the yard I threw the reins on to the pony's shivering neck and rushed into the kitchen. My mother and Billy were there. They stood up and looked at me silently. I had meant to blurt out the whole story, to say that I would be gone in three days and home again with my father a week after that, but the look of long patience in my mother's face made me pause. How cruel it would be to raise her hopes, to let her stake all her faith on my adventure! I tried to speak casually as I told my story, though my face must have belied me.

Billy took his lead from me and when I had finished he said, as casually:

"It all sounds rather promising. It's a good time of the year for a sail."

My mother said:

"Mr. Conway must be a very good man. To give a boat, and to send his own man as well—I didn't know there was so much goodness in the world!"

This embarrassed me a little, as Matt Raftery's face came up before me. But I hoped she would never see his little foxy eyes, at least until we would have returned from our voyage. So I only said:

"Of course Pat expects to get some of whatever there

is on the island, as his reward. If there is anything," I added.

"He'll deserve that, at least," said my mother.

"So Bartley recognized the little tools as Tomeen's," said Billy. "That proves that Mikus's story was true. He could not have made it all up."

My mother was looking at me doubtfully. Now she turned to Billy and said:

"I don't know what to say to it all. There's Jim went off and never came back, and now Michael is to go, and I may never see him again. Can you tell me—am I to let him go? Only tell me to do it, and I won't say another word."

Poor Billy was in a fix. He saw those trusting eyes on him, and he knew that he must make a decision that would, perhaps, leave my mother alone for the rest of her life. But he had made up his mind what was best to be done, and nothing could shake him. He looked at me critically, out of the corners of his eyes, till I felt myself going red in the face.

"I't s like this, ma'am," he said. "Michael is a fine big lad, used to a man's work, and he has had a man's responsibility before now. Well, if he goes off and gets drowned, it will be because he was too silly to save himself. And if he's too silly to save himself, then it's worth no one else's while to save him, for he'll only live to get into some other trouble later on!"

"Ha!" thought I. "I'd like to see you philosophizing like that to one of those big waves that go about outside the islands, looking for little boats full of people to devour!"

But Billy knew what he was doing. My mother wrinkled her forehead while she considered what he had said, and at last she said quietly:

"Very well. That's exactly what Bartley said about Jim."

From that moment on she was as good as her word, and never again mentioned her fears for my safety.

We spent the whole evening in making plans for the farm and for my departure. My mother promised to provide clothes for Joe, too, because Mrs. Pete would be too busy now to do anything for him, she said. She was already planning to give us enough fisherman's jerseys for a year's voyage. The women in the islands made, and still make, a kind of closely knitted jersey, with an intricate pattern for extra thickness, and with so much of the natural oil remaining in the wool as to make it almost waterproof. I could see that we were not going to be neglected in the matter of clothes, at any rate, for we were to get no less than three of these each!

I remember well how I tossed all night from wave to wave of my bed, what leering sharks pursued me through underwater caverns, where red-eyed monsters lurked and the bones of dead ships lay, until I reached an island of leprachauns, each with a crock of gold, whom I chased unrelenting over rock and briar, but who always eluded me. Little green grinning faces! How I hated them! How I grasped at their flashing coat-tails and tried to trip them by every means I knew, until the morning sun came to release me from my torment.

I got up brightly enough, however, and was soon getting ready for the road. My mother packed some eggs and butter into the cart for Mrs. Pete, and I was off. Joe was to have told Mrs. Pete our plan last night, and I hoped it had been as well received as had my story.

When I reached the town, I found that Pete had been taken to hospital the night before, and Mrs. Pete had just gone to visit him.

"I was up there early," said Joe, "and he's much better to-day."

He said he had told Mrs. Pete about Pat Conway's

offer, and she had answered him in almost the same terms that Billy had used about me.

"If all the good food you have eaten in the last few years hasn't made a sensible man of you, you may as well go out and drown, for you're not worth feeding any more."

Of course she said that we must not go alone. She knew Matt Raftery well for a slinking little fox, and Pat Conway was not much better, but she could not see what they could do to injure us. They were good sailors too. And she thought we were very lucky to have found anyone to lend us a boat.

This was great news. Now the way seemed quite clear. I waited while Joe brought in turf and potatoes for Mrs. Pete, and tidied the kitchen against her return. At last we were off down the quay, across the little canal and into the yard. At the gate we paused to draw long breaths to calm our pounding hearts, before advancing up the yard to where Matt was again wielding his paint brush. He put it down when he saw us coming, and went to call Pat from the office. Pat led us to the boat that he had shown us yesterday.

"There she is," he said, "a sister ship to O'Neill's own boat. She's had many names in her day—Daisy and Mary Ann, and Cormorant, and once she was called after a strange bird that doesn't be in these parts at all—Kiwi, it was. She has no name now."

I looked where the name should have been, and could only see faint black lines that had been heavily painted over with white paint.

"I know what we'll call her," I said. "The Wave-Rider!"

"That's a queer class of a name," said Matt sourly. "Who ever heard of a boat with a name like that?"

And he spat into the canal in disgust.

"That must be her name," said I in determination.

"A boat shouldn't have a fancy name like that," said Matt. "The next thing you know she'll be called the 'Jockey'!" He laughed raucously. "Wave-Rider indeed! 'Kate', or 'Jane', or 'Molly' is the right kind of a name for a boat, the way you can say what you like to her, the same as you would to your wife!"

"All the same," said Pat, pacifically, "Michael has the right to name the boat, since he's directing the expedition."

And he signalled to Matt to hold his tongue.

I was pleased with this little victory. Naming the boat made me feel that I owned her already. The name, of course, was the name of the boat that had reached Inishmanann long ago, according to old Bartley.

"No time to be lost now," said Pat heartily. "You must get to work on her at once, and no slacking!"

We were only too eager to begin, and he soon had us scraping and sandpapering the hull, in preparation for painting.

As we worked I began to feel a glow of affection for the boat. She was made of teak, dark and hard as granite. The work was slow, but very satisfying, and Pat commended us when he came to look at our progress at dinner-time.

We had dinner with Mrs. Pete in her warm, comfortable kitchen, and then we rushed back to our labours as fast as we could. But Pat and Matt were more leisurely. They had shut the gates, and we had to kick our heels outside until they returned.

We spent the afternoon at the same work as we had done in the morning. Matt climbed on board and began some repairs to the cabin. He hauled up some short teak planks by a rope, and we could hear his saw singing and his hammer ringing as he worked. After a while Pat went out of the yard, and as soon as he was gone Matt put his head over the side and called out:

"Hi, you, small fellow! Come up here and hold the nails for me!"

Joe climbed on board and went into the cabin. It seemed that Matt only wanted his company, for he gave him very little work to do. I heard none of their conversation, but Joe said afterwards that it was very entertaining. Matt talked of pirates and smugglers and every other water-thief that ever was, but he would not say for certain that he had been any of these things himself. He did not try to pump Joe, for he was too busy describing his own clevernesses. All the time he was talking he went on with his carpentry. He fitted in the planks as carefully as if he were building an expensive cruising yacht, for he said that there is only one right way to do a job. He explained that the new boards would have to be french-polished on the inside and painted on the outside. Joe was idle all this time, except when he handed Matt a tool for which he could very well have reached himself. It was irritating to have time wasted like this, but when Joe picked up a nail to drive it himself, Matt turned on him so savagely that he dropped it at once.

"There's going to be no botched job on this ship!" he snarled.

We were both despairing when Pat's step was heard outside the yard.

"Quick! Over the side!" Matt hissed. "Not by the ladder, you little fool! The other side!"

Joe dropped over the side away from the gate just as Pat came through, and took up his sandpapering where he had left off. Pat came over to inspect our work.

"Not much work done for the time," he said. "You'll want to look livelier than that, or you won't be ready this side of Christmas."

"Too young, too small," said Matt contemptuously from the deck.

We could say nothing to that. We went to work more vigorously than ever, and we had a good part of the hull cleaned by the time it became too dark for work. As we left it, I smoothed my hand lovingly over the wood, and felt as proud as if I had built the whole boat myself.

So it was every day. Pat taught me how to use a blow-lamp, and how to make the joinings between the planks watertight. There were a hundred other things to be learned, and gradually we came to feel that we knew our boat like an old friend. We polished her till she shone, and we tightened every screw in the length and breadth of her. We made a new mainsail and mended the old ones. This was the part I liked best, sitting there in the sun of the lengthening days, pulling my needle in and out and dreaming of vast oceans. I could almost feel the rock of the waves as I sat there.

By the time we had reached this task, the rest of the boat was finished. Pat would start us off in the morning and then leave us for a long time, while Matt went on with his work on other boats. Sometimes when they were far enough away, we would talk quietly about our plans. We were determined on one thing by now, that Matt was not going to be of the party. As we had worked together he had become more and more arrogant. He was the leader of the expedition, he said, and the captain of the ship. He always said "When we sail out," but he always said too, "When I sail home." We took this to mean that he had already been instructed by Pat to leave us on the island or dispose of us by some other means as soon as we had found the treasure. Matt was not clever enough to conceal the plot from us.

Pat, on the other hand, was as smooth and sweet as a bowl of cream. He talked of the future when we would be driving around the town in glory. He said we would become great business-men, and that everyone would respect us. He said he would be proud to tell everyone that he had had a very small share in our rise to fame. He seemed never to notice our silence when he spoke like this. We were thinking how glad we were that he had not planned to come with us himself, because we knew he would be more than a match for us. And he was too big. Matt was quite a small man, and therefore much better suited to our purpose.

The boat was to be launched through the little canal and tied up in the dock. There was a row of old warehouses there, long gone out of use. Joe knew every one of these as well as he knew his own house, and he said that in one of them there was a big cellar. A trap-door in the corner of the ground-floor room led, by a flight of steps, into the cellar. Our plan was simply to attack Matt and bring him somehow to this cellar and imprison him there. Then we would sail away by night when no one was watching. Joe had put a new bolt on the trap-door, and we were trusting to luck that Matt would not be too strong for us.

There were two big drawbacks in this plan. One was that we would have to manage the boat alone, but we felt that with a little experience we would learn enough to be fairly safe. The other was more serious. There was to be a small engine in the boat, to be used only in emergencies. I guessed that this engine would be very important for landing on Inishmanann, if we ever got there. Pat had talked a good deal about the danger of fire, so it seemed unlikely that he would put the petrol on board until the moment before we sailed. If he did not, it looked as if we would have to depend solely on our sails.

At last, one evening we were done. The little ship was a beautiful sight to see, standing there on her blocks with every inch of her in perfect trim. Below the water-line she was scarlet, and above she was as white as a swan. Her rails and cabin door were brown. Her ropes, or sheets, as

I was learning to call them, were all new, and with her new sail as well, I thought she would look very grand in the water.

We all stood around her to admire.

"She looks good," said Pat. "She's a credit to you all." He turned to Joe and me. "Now you run along home, and we'll launch her in the morning."

We went out of the yard together, quite speechless with excitement. I remember how long the road home seemed that evening, I was so anxious to tell that our labours were finished at last. It had only taken four weeks, but our impatience had made it seem much longer.

I hardly slept a wink all night, and with the dawn I was ready to be off again. My mother had two bundles of clothes ready, one for each of us, and I was to leave them at Joe's house.

At his door, Joe was jumping from one foot to the other, waiting for me. Mrs. Pete made me come in, and open the two parcels. She was very pleased with what my mother had provided.

"Oh, the fine jerseys!" she said, lifting them up."And socks enough for an army. Now I'll get you sea-boots and oilskins and you'll be ready for anything."

"But we won't want oilskins in the summer," I said. "In a week it will be May, and the weather will be warm and mild."

"I'm not supposed to know anything about the sea," said Mrs. Pete, "though I'm all my life to listening to talk about it. And the thing everyone agrees about is that it's wet. It has a way of coming in over the side when you least expect it, and when that's not happening, there's rain falling. It would be a poor sailor would put to sea without oilskins and sea-boots."

"I'm afraid I'm a dry-land sailor," I said.

"So am I," said Mrs. Pete tartly, "but I'm a good one!"

And so she was. Her advice about food and clothes were invaluable, as we afterwards found.

Presently we left her and went down to the yard. It was still very early, but Pat and Matt were both there. Word had got around that a boat would be launched that morning, and half a dozen men had arrived to help and give advice, both good and bad. I could see that Pat was annoyed at attracting so much attention. He must have known, however, that in a small port like ours, everything that happens is interesting and important. He did not dare to turn the men away, so he was making a pretence of hearty gratitude to them. But there was a wicked little glint in his eye that showed he was really in a bad temper.

The leader of the so-called helpers was a tall young man called Tomsy. He was dressed in a navy-blue suit, as clean as if it had never been worn before. He had a new furry tweed cap, of which he was very careful. He dusted a box with his hand and laid the cap on it, and warded off everyone who came near with outspread hands and a cry of:

"Mind my new cap!"

When the others ran to help bring out the big wooden rollers, he followed at a little distance with encouraging remarks, but he never put his hands on anything dirty. The men all laughed at him, but they did what he told them for all that.

One thing they all agreed on, that Joe and I were both too young to know anything about launching boats. They pushed us back out of the way, and told us not to fall into the canal, and made us run messages, so that neither of us got a proper view of what was happening. At last they all stood back, and there was the *Wave-Rider* afloat in the little canal, erect and trim as a little battleship.

Now Matt tied a line to the boat, to tow it down the canal. Joe climbed on board, and without a word, I followed him. The helpers ran ahead to open the lock gates, and presently we sailed through into the dock. Joe looked at me, and I could see that we both felt that this was the first stage of our journey, that it had begun at last.

When we were tied up to the quay wall, the men hung about for a while. They were obviously waiting to see what would happen next. Pat strolled away towards the town, as if he had no more interest in the boat, and Matt went back to work in the yard. Joe and I did not know what to do, so we just sat there in the sun. Presently the men drifted away one by one, until at last we were alone.

Then as if by magic, Pat was back.

"I thought they would never go," he said sourly. "Come along out of that! There's plenty of work still to be done. Some people have long necks and long tongues, and it's well to get ahead with the work while they're gone."

He herded us into the yard, and down to a shed we had never before seen open.

"I'm my own chandler," he said with a sly smile. "It's often convenient to be able to stock a ship on the quiet, or to keep a shy friend here for a few days unknown to anyone."

There was a fine supply of food there, to be sure. We got to work at once, carrying some of it down to the boat —a bag of flaked oatmeal, two bags of potatoes, tins of soup and meat.

"You won't be able to cook much," said Pat. "Porridge and potatoes will be the most of your diet. And who knows how long you may have to stay on the island before you come back loaded with gold."

He looked at me meaningly, and I could see that he was hoping for some information. I said nothing. He gripped me by the shoulder and put his face close to mine, showing his sharp yellow teeth in a snarl.

"I'm staking a lot on you, young man," he hissed. "My

best boat and my man—if you don't come home with something worth while, it will be the worse for you."

"If I come home at all I'll be satisfied," I said. "I can promise that you'll have a share of anything that we bring."

We put a big water-barrel into the cabin, in the bows, and Pat showed us how to secure the bung. He gave us an old oilskin sheet too, to save our supply of water, and an extra water-barrel. We took tools for repairs, and a great coil of new rope, and a pick-axe. I made no comment on these last, for I knew they were meant for digging up buried treasure and hauling it to the boat. Pat added a few empty sacks, and I almost felt sorry for him. One could see that he was already counting golden guineas. I wondered if we were cheating him in taking his boat at all, and then I remembered Bartley's old story about the island.

"Who knows but Pat may be right after all?" I said to myself.

And I stored his treasure-hunting equipment carefully by the water-barrel.

He was back at his usual song again, about our being such good lads, and how happy he was to serve us.

When we were fully loaded, the boat was still high out of the water. Pat looked into the little hold.

"Some more ballast wanted here," he said.

Then I saw that the ballast was not big stones, as in the islanders' boats, nor pig-lead, as in some of the yachts, but water stored in casks.

"Stones drag you down, but water holds you up," Pat explained. "Water-ballast floats if the boat fills. Stones sink you."

Last of all he brought from his office the neatest little brass-mounted compass I had ever seen. Matt brought screws and screwed it by the helm.

"And that is the last job done," said Pat. "Now perhaps you will tell us what you know about the island."

I was sorely tempted to tell him the little I knew, he looked so friendly. But I hardened my heart and remembered that on me alone depended the rescue of my father.

"Just before we sail I'll tell you," I said firmly. "That was the bargain."

Pat seemed to swell up, until I thought he would burst with rage. I moved back from the quay wall, lest he knock me into the water. But gradually he subsided, and forced out his usual smile, and we left him with a great show of friendliness.

⋆ VII ⋆

It was late afternoon by now, and Joe and I were both tired, but very contented. Mrs. Pete had a meal ready for us, and while we ate we had to tell her about what food we had stored on the boat, and how much. She nodded when I repeated Pat's remark about the smallness of the cooking space.

"I'll make you some scones that will do you for the first part of the journey," she said. "You must eat them before the salt gets into them."

"You don't think much of the sea, Mrs. Pete," I said.

"I do not, then," she said. "It's too independent. But with Matt you'll be all right. And you must go when your father sent for you."

I could see that she was uneasy about us, and my conscience pricked me for not telling her what we planned to do with Matt. But I knew that would mean the end of our voyage, so I said nothing. Joe was silent too. He was to leave a letter telling her where to find Matt after we had gone, so that he would not starve in his underground prison.

Soon I was on my way home for the last time. I was to spend the day there, and in the evening Joe and I were to go down to the boat where we were to sleep, with Matt, so as to be ready for an early start next morning. As I drove along I looked with affection at each landmark by the roadside. I wanted to fill my mind with memories to bring with me on the voyage.

Billy had walked a little way to meet me, and we drove back to the house together. As we went I told him about the end of the work, but when we reached home we spoke no more of boats. All that evening, and the next day, not a word was said about our voyage, and when evening came I drove off with only the same farewells as if I were going to market.

Billy was to fetch the pony from town the next day, and I drove at once to the stable where he was to stay. I stroked his nose and patted his neck before leaving him, and I fancied there was a sorrowful note in his answering whinny.

Down at the quay, Joe was in his little den. All the cages were open and the animals and birds gone.

"I let them all go," he said. "I could not be sure they would be fed properly while I'm away. They are all well enough to look after themselves by now."

"Was the rat sorry to go?" I asked.

"It's funny you should ask that," said Joe. "I know he was quite well, but he didn't seem to want his freedom at all. He went very slowly over to the quay wall and down the steps to the water. He kept looking back at me and rubbing his mouth with one paw. I went after him and lifted him up to see if he was hurt, but he was not. I dropped him into the water from the steps, and he swam very slowly out to the red mooring buoy there." He pointed with his finger. "He's sitting there still, looking at me," he finished gloomily.

"He was remembering the fine food you gave him," I said. "He knows he hasn't much chance of getting hot scones and butter on his own."

He was a character, that rat. I could see him there, sitting on the buoy, and managing to look quite lonesome and pathetic, though he was so far off. It was something about the way he hunched up his shoulders.

Suddenly Joe sat up.

"Michael! Let's bring the rat with us! He won't eat much. I can give him some of my own food."

I did not know what to say. I most certainly did not want to live with Joe's rat, especially on a small boat.

"But if the boat goes down he'll be drowned," I said desperately. "It's all right for us, because we know what we're doing. But it would not be fair to bring a poor innocent rat with us, at the risk of his life."

"He could swim," said Joe doubtfully.

"He couldn't swim very far," I said. "It would be all right if we were near land, but supposing we go down in the middle of the Atlantic Ocean? Then he would certainly be drowned. You would not like to be the cause of his death."

"You're quite right," said Joe. "You're much more thoughtful for him than I am. And he may still be here when we come back."

"You may be sure he'll find you when we come back," I said with relief.

Mrs. Pete had had to go away for the day, so the house was empty when we got there. Joe had been to the hospital in the morning, to see Pete, and had got his blessing on our adventure. And like everyone else, he had said we would be safe with Matt, because he was a good sailor.

We took our bundles of clothes and went down to the boat. The sun was going down in a bed of scarlet and grey, and the water shone like gold. We threw our bundles down on to the deck and jumped down after them. Matt's head came out of the cabin, and was withdrawn again. In a moment Pat came out, smiling affably.

"Well, well! All here on time, ready for anything!" He rubbed his hands and beamed at us. "You're to sleep on board to-night, of course, but first you must have a meal. Yes, we must celebrate, eh, Matt?"

Matt grinned evilly, and nodded.

"You're to come to my own house, where my wife is ready for you, and you can come back here afterwards. Just put away your things and come along."

Now that we were on the boat, I did not want to leave it again, but there was no help for it. Pat saw our hesitation and instructed Matt to stay on board.

"And keep a good eye on her. She's a valuable craft."

Again Matt made no reply but his evil grin.

With a hand on each of our shoulders, Pat led us up the quay to his house. It was a small two-story house with green blinds and a green door. Lace curtains hid the inside, and the brass door-handle and knocker were polished till they shone.

"Ah, here we are," said Pat, somewhat too loudly and heartily.

His wife must have been watching for our arrival, for she opened the door just then and asked us to come in. It was hard for me to decide why it was that I disliked and feared her. She spoke very softly and sweetly, and she moved about as silently as a cat. Now and then, in a pause in the talk, she would turn up her eyes and say: "Ah, yes-s-s!" in a sibilant undertone. It had nothing to do with the conversation, and every time she did it I got the creeps. It was as if she was mourning for someone who had just died. And still the smile never left her face. She made a great show of friendliness to us. She plied us with food and drink, and said what brave boys we were. She said we were going to have a good voyage, that she felt it in her bones, and the weather looked settled. She said we were to bring her back a parrot, ha-ha, she had always wanted a parrot.

Her talk made my head buzz, and I thought with longing of my quiet gentle mother. I laid my head back on my chair and closed my eyes for a moment. When I opened them I noticed that Joe seemed to be asleep. Pat was standing up, looking at us both, and he was not smiling now. I tried to stand up, but my legs would not hold me, so that I fell back into my chair again.

Pat's wife bent over me.

"Are you not feeling well? Come and lie down, and you'll feel better."

Her smile was as wide as a church door, and I closed my eyes for a second to shut it out.

"You drugged me," I said, and then my tongue would do no more work for me.

I had to lie there glaring at her helplessly, while she went through a whole pretence of innocence.

"Pat, Pat! Did you hear what he said? Oh, he must be sick! How could he think of such a thing?"

Then suddenly I was unconscious, and I heard no more. I wonder now how long she went on with her pantomime before she realized that she was wasting her time.

To this day I do not know where we spent the night. It was daylight when I woke up, and on the instant I saw that we were in Pat's office in the boatyard. Joe was lying on the floor beside me, and as I watched him, he groaned a little and began to wake up.

We only had time to tell each other that our heads ached before Pat opened the door. When he saw that we were awake he came in, and now he was smiling again.

"You're just in time," he said. "The boat is all ready to go, and we're waiting on the crew."

We dragged ourselves to our feet and followed him outside. Judging by the sun, I thought it must be very early morning.

"Now, don't blame me for what I did," said Pat. "It was all for your own good. Young lads do be foolish, and I thought you might have some idea of going alone."

I felt sick with disappointment. Of course he must have

guessed that we meant to leave Matt behind. I wondered how he had done it. As if he knew what I was thinking he went on:

"I said to myself: 'If I was a young lad, what would I do? I'd get away in the night somehow, when no one was noticing.' Now maybe you had no such idea, but I thought it better to make sure we have no mistakes. I wouldn't like to think of the two of you out on the wide ocean alone."

As we followed him through the yard I made up my mind that we must go on with the voyage in spite of Pat's trick. We might never again get a chance of a boat if we withdrew now. Joe walked along without a word, but when I caught his eye he nodded, ever so little. He wanted to go ahead too.

"It's a pity we both have headaches on the first day out," I said, "for I'm afraid we won't be a very useful crew."

"That will be all right," said Pat. "Matt will understand. It's easy sailing inside the bay, and by the time you get outside Fort Island you'll be feeling better."

There was not a soul on the quays. There was a pleasant south-westerly breeze, not too stiff, and the sky was clear and cloudless. Matt was in the boat, making ready to hoist the sails, and he leered at us as we climbed unsteadily aboard. Now that we were ready, Pat was in a great hurry to have us gone. He bustled up and down loosening the ropes that tied the boat to two bollards on the quay wall, and then he coiled the ropes and flung them aboard. His eyes darted up the quay towards the houses all the time, as if he were afraid someone would come before we were off. While Matt held on to the wall with a boat-hook, Pat barked:

"Now, young man! Your course, please!"

I told them then about my theory of setting a course

straight through the mouth of the bay from the Eagle's Rock, and about the old story of sailing for seven days and seven nights. As I knew nothing about the sea, I thought they must find this too vague to be useful, but to my surprise they did not. They consulted together for a few minutes, and then Pat gave Matt long and close instructions. Matt got angry at the suggestion that he was not the better seaman, and they shouted at one another for a while. Then they made it up, and finally reached some kind of agreement. I only understood a little of their talk, but Joe seemed to understand it all. Joe was quite at home on the sea.

At last Matt gave a long shove with the boat-hook, so that we floated out into the middle of the dock. Then he and Joe hoisted the sails. They filled with wind and we began to move. Joe took the helm, and we sailed out of the dock on the high tide. I watched Pat's figure on the quay grow smaller and smaller, until he looked as if a passing dog could have eaten him in one bite.

I remember how small the town looked from the sea, just a few houses huddled together with the fields stretching away up behind them. Across the bay, the high blue hills seemed very far away. As we passed the lighthouse, the lightkeeper waved to us from his tower. He lived on his little island all the year round, and to him the town and the docks always looked as they did to us now. There was not another boat in sight, and I wondered where the fishing boats had gone. When I asked Joe, he said that they were probably outside Fort Island. They often spent several days out there. If the weather became stormy, they would run into one of the little island harbours for shelter. Here the fishermen met all the foreign trawlermen who had come for shelter like themselves, and they spent the time, till the storm blew itself out, in comparing the different ports of the world.

When we were clear of the lighthouse, Matt got out a map and calculated closely what course we should take. He sat by Joe at the helm and they consulted over it together. Then Matt said grudgingly:

"You know something about boats, sure enough. But as for that fellow," he jerked his thumb in my direction, "he would be better at home at his mother's washtub!"

He laughed raucously, and I felt myself getting red in the face. I knew that what he said was very nearly true.

Now Matt took over the helm from Joe. He stood a moment looking at us, and then he said:

"Come here, boys. Come closer."

We came closer, until we stood one on either side of him. He leered at us triumphantly, nodding his head and making grimaces. This went on for perhaps a minute before he said:

"Now I have an announcement to make."

He paused the more to impress us, and then he roared suddenly:

"I am the captain of this ship, and there is to be no manner of doubt about that! Do you know what the captain's job is?"

I said I supposed he is in charge of the ship.

"That's right. And he has power of life and death over the crew. Life—and death!"

Suddenly he had whipped a wicked-looking long knife out of his pocket. He held it up between us, so that the sun flashed on its blade. I could not help starting back from it, and at this Matt looked very pleased.

He spoke to his knife.

"He's afraid of you, Sally, my dear. Sally is her name, you see," he explained to us. "Sally is a good girl, devoted to her duty. She has tasted blood before now, and she's always hungry for a little more. We give her some now and then, just to keep her happy. Don't we, my Sally?"

I was fascinated by this talk, so much so that I am sure I would not have been surprised if the knife had answered him.

He thumbed the blade lovingly.

"A good knife is like a dog that way. Once a dog tastes blood it's hard to satisfy him with anything less."

I wished he would stop talking about blood. He waved the knife under our noses, enjoying his feeling of power over us.

"You may think I'm a bit old-fashioned to use a knife, but a knife has more personality than a gun, and it don't talk so loud."

I had come to the conclusion that he was not going to kill us just then, so I said:

"Her owner talks enough for two!"

Quick as lightning, he had the knife at my throat. I could feel the steel tickling me. One lurch of the boat and I was lost. Joe stood as though turned to stone, afraid that if he moved Matt would make an end of me. In a moment Matt lowered the knife.

"No back-answers to the captain, you young pup!" he said. "I have a quick way with people like you. Over the side to fatten the fishes. And how I'd cry when I'd be telling your mother how your foot slipped and you fell overboard before I could save you! And Joe, here, how he lost his life trying to haul you out! I can cry like a baby whenever I want to. Look!"

And he wrinkled up his face and let out two big tears. I almost laughed in spite of our predicament.

I could imagine the scene quite well. I thought Matt and Pat might even have rehearsed it together. It looked as if our early impression was the right one, and that Matt had received instructions not to bring us home at all.

However, this did not seem a good time to start a fight. We were still too near land, for one thing, and we might be seen from the shore. And it seemed that our chances of success might be more if we took Matt unawares. Just now he was darting a sharp eye from one to the other of us, watching for an attack.

I made a helpless gesture.

"We don't mind if you're the captain," I said. "You're a better sailor than either of us, and I, for one, will be glad to learn what I can from you."

Joe agreed with this, and I could see by his expression that he understood my idea. I was glad of this, for I was sure that I would get little or no opportunity from now on of conspiring with him.

Matt put away his knife again, and said:

"Now we know where we are. From now on my orders are the law!"

He handed over the helm to Joe again, and began to teach me how to handle the sails. I got lost in a bog of nautical terms, and after the first time I was afraid to ask what they meant.

"When I say luff I mean LUFF!" he roared in answer to my timid question.

I expected to see Sally come hopping out of his pocket again. But though his hand went in that direction, he stopped and went into the cabin muttering.

The *Wave-Rider* was a lively boat, and by noon we had travelled halfway along the bay. We were ravenously hungry by then, but we did not want to be the first to mention food. Matt sat sprawling amidships, snarling out orders from time to time, and cursing our clumsiness. He had brought out one of the brandy-bottles we had for emergencies and now and then he would pull out the cork and swallow a nip of the neat spirit. His eyes popped a little every time he did it.

At last he sent me into the cabin to prepare a meal, with the remark that a sissy like me should be a good cook.

I boiled some potatoes on the oil-stove and we ate them with tinned meat and some of Mrs. Pete's scones. I felt my courage rise again, and Joe, too, looked more dangerous. He had gone about his work all morning without a word, but with his black eyebrows drawing closer and closer together, as Matt's jibes made him angrier.

Soon after we had finished our meal, the wind dropped. It had turned out a brilliantly sunny day, with a clear blue sky, and a haze by the distant shore. Now the sea became silkily smooth, and the sails flapped loosely from the mast. We made very little way for a while, and then we seemed to stop moving altogether.

We could have used our engine, of course, but we did not want to waste petrol. Matt told us to keep watch, and tell him when the breeze would come up again, which it would certainly do in the evening. Then he applied himself to his brandy bottle again.

Joe and I sat in the stern together. The tall shadow of the sail saved us from the heat of the sun, and in any other circumstances it would have been quite pleasant sitting there. As the afternoon wore on, we drew closer and closer together, and our eyes never left Matt. He was getting drowsy now, and seemed to have lost all his watchfulness. No one spoke a word, and gradually we saw his head go lower and lower until at last he was asleep.

Joe nudged me, and then went creeping forward. I followed as silently as I could. Joe reached Matt and bent over him. On the instant Matt's eyes opened.

My heart stood still. Joe threw himself on top of Matt where he lay, and panted:

"The rope! Get the rope!"

I seized it, a new coil that hung by the cabin door, with its end hanging loose. We had marked it well earlier.

Only for that loose end we could never have captured him. He wriggled like an eel. He was an experienced fighter, and a grown man, and though there were two of us, we were only boys. I got the rope about his legs and pulled, and somehow I managed to tie a slip knot on it. After that it was easy. We soon had him trussed up, and Joe had his friend Sally stowed away safely in his pocket. Then we stood up and looked at him. Joe said:

"We didn't start this kind of thing. But you left us no choice."

Matt glared at us venomously, but he said nothing. I was surprised at this, for I had expected a stream of wicked language from him. Then all at once I saw the reason for his silence. He was afraid. He was so frightened that he was shaking.

This was a piece of luck, and Joe was quick to take advantage of it. He took Matt's knife out of his pocket again and swung it by the blade before its owner's nose.

"There she is, your Sally. Only she's working for me now. And if you call for help, or raise a row as we come near Fort Island, Sally will have her wish and taste blood again. And how I'll cry when I'm telling anyone that's interested how we had to throw you overboard because you were too dangerous!"

Matt licked his lips and croaked:

"You'd never do that—you'd never do a thing like that!"

"We would," said I, hoping that I sounded as if I meant it. "We would if you forced us to. Someone's life depends on this expedition of ours, and we must consider which is the more valuable, yours or his."

"I won't cause any trouble," Matt whined, "only don't throw me overboard all tied up like this."

We both shuddered at the very thought of doing such a thing, but we tried to look as if it would have cost us nothing. We supposed that Matt was in the habit of treating his enemies as callously as that, and it behoved us to

appear to be a match for him in this as well as in everything else.

"Don't put ideas into our heads," I said casually.

We heaved him into the cabin and shut the door on him. Then we went to the stern to confer. The evening was coming on now, and a few clouds had appeared. Soon a breeze would come up, Joe said, and we could reach Fort Island after dark. We meant to bring Matt ashore and leave him on the island, and continue at once on our way, alone.

★ VIII ★

It was not long before the expected breeze came. At first it ruffled the water lightly and passed on, but soon it settled down to a steady brisk breeze that set the water lapping at the bows and sent us tacking on towards Fort Island. Joe said it was a common thing inside the bay for the wind to drop for a whole day.

"But once we're beyond the island it's more likely to be a little too good for us."

We were only just able to handle the boat together. We began to wonder what would happen if we ran into rough weather, and how we were going to find time to sleep.

"Just think of the people who have sailed the Atlantic alone in boats much smaller than this," said Joe.

I thought of them, experienced sailors all.

"Well, each of us must learn to handle the boat alone," said Joe.

"You can do that already," said I. "But what about me? If I have to start climbing the mast while I'm holding the helm——"

"One doesn't climb the mast of this kind of boat," said Joe. "Look, it's as easy as driving a horse—"

And he began again to teach me about boats until my head was so full of information that it would not hold it all.

"Don't sail too near the wind."

I did not know I was doing it—I could not see the wind.

"Keep your boat full."

Not of water, as you might expect, but of wind!

"Luff up to beam gusts, then put up your helm and let the boat come back."

It was Greek to me until I had done it several times.

Tacking was a nightmare at first. While Joe did it, it seemed quite simple. But the first time I took over, I thought I had tacked us all into Kingdom Come. I brought her round in a beautiful curve, till her head came into the wind. Then suddenly Joe leaped on the helm and jammed it over. My heart pounded with fright.

"You have to get her past head of wind," he roared into my ear. "Now ease your helm to amidships."

I did, and the boom swung across.

"That's all," said Joe. "Quite easy, isn't it?"

"Quite easy," said I faintly.

Fort Island was the most westerly of the islands. As we came close, we could see its high ridge crowned with the prehistoric fort that had given it its name. There was a level part at the side that looked towards the bay, and here was Kilbricken, the island's biggest village. It had a little deep-water quay, where the steamer from the mainland called twice a week. The quay and the curve of the shore made a harbour where the lifeboat was anchored, and where the little Spanish trawlers came in for eggs and potatoes which they bought from the islanders.

We did not think of landing at Kilbricken; it was too populous for us. But around the point there was another quay and another little harbour, where we hoped we would not excite so much curiosity. The few scattered houses there could hardly be called a village. An old Cromwellian fortress rose straight out of the water by the quay, cutting off a view of the boats from all except those who came down specially to see them. Joe said the name of this place was Kilkieran, which means Saint Kieran's cell.

As we approached the quay, darkness fell. Little points

of light appeared in the cottage windows by the shore, and at intervals all along the top of the ridge that ran the whole length of the island. This was where the road was, and it was easy to follow its course by the lights.

There were no lights to lead us into the little harbour, but Joe had eyes like a cat, and he knew the way. I marvelled at the ease with which he was able to steer us in, in the heavy dark. At the right moment we lowered our sails, and soon we were gliding along by the quay wall. Joe slowed our progress with the boat-hook against the wall, and at last we were secured to an iron ring that hung from it. The tide was high, and he skipped ashore with another rope at once.

It was very quiet in the harbour. Here and there about us there were patches of heavier blackness, showing that there were other boats there too. In some of these a faint glow came from the hatches. They were hookers, like Pete's boat, and it looked as if the men were spending the night on board.

As soon as we were tied up, heads began to pop up against the glow, and voices asked us, in Irish, who we were. We answered in the same language, and they wished the blessings of heaven on us. We knew then that they were the island boats, perhaps planning to go out fishing later on. The men asked us for news of the town, and one of them wanted to know the price of young pigs at the last fair. We chatted to them in a leisurely way, as if we had nothing else to do, and were glad of the company. We hoped that Matt was still afraid of us, and that he would not betray his presence by a shout. At last, one by one, the heads went down again. We waited for a long time until all was quiet. Then Joe slipped into the cabin.

He loosened the ropes on Matt's legs and led him out, having warned him to be quiet. Then we made him climb ashore. Joe pressed the knife to his back, and we hustled him silently along the pier to the road. We followed the road for a piece until we came to a stile.

We went through the stile and found ourselves in a rocky field that stretched upwards to the sky.

"Somewhere up there, there is a little stone cell," said Joe. "It belonged to Saint Kieran, who had a monastery here about the time of Saint Patrick, or a little later. I was there once with Pete, long ago."

I knew these little cells well, for they were to be found here and there on the mainland too. The ones I had seen were very small, perhaps eight feet by four, and their walls and roofs were about two feet thick. There was usually only one door, and no window, so that one could not imagine a more effective prison. There were many such cells on the island, I had always heard, for it had once been a favourite retreat for hermits and saints.

So we began the search for the cell, and it was like some strange frightful dream. We fell into holes and over boulders, and we climbed loose stone walls that crashed in heaps about us. Every moment we expected to be challenged. And always we climbed upwards, hoping that from the top of the hill we would be able to pick out the shadow of the little cell against the sky.

The fields of the island were covered with glacial boulders, and the islanders cultivated what little land there was in a kind of crazy pattern between the rocks. We leaped over these rocks and walked round them until my knees gave way.

"We'll have to rest for a moment," I panted, and I sat down on the ground.

Suddenly Matt, who had not spoken a word since we had left the boat, took courage and said:

"There's some sort of a house up there behind us."

"It's the cell!" said Joe. "Come on!"

We stumbled on until we reached the little doorway

in what looked like a heap of rocks. It was no more than four feet high. The islanders had made a wooden door for it to keep the animals out, because it was a holy place. There was an iron bar to hold it in position.

"I hope Saint Kieran won't mind," said Joe, as we pushed Matt inside.

"But I'll never be found," whined Matt. "I'll die here!"

"You will not," said Joe. "You may be sure that the man who owns the land will guess that something has happened here, and he'll come up and let you out in the morning. The islanders always find out things like that."

With this doubtful comfort we left him, and started off down the hill. The going was even slower than on the way up, though we had the lights of the houses below to guide us. It seemed that we had stumbled downhill for hours before we came at last to the stile, and climbed out on to the road again.

"Now we can really start our search for the island," said Joe.

I tried to make some cheerful answer, but I was full of fears for our future. With Matt's help we might have found the island, but I thought that Joe and I might sail up and down the North Atlantic for years without ever even sighting it. Still I could not regret our having got rid of Matt, for we knew now that our lives were in danger as long as we had him with us.

Suddenly I clutched Joe's arm and whispered:

"Do you hear that?"

He stopped to listen. Up to now, our feet crunching the sand had been the only sound in the stillness. But now the tick-tick-tick of an engine could be heard, growing louder every second.

"It's just a motor-boat—perhaps a trawler," said Joe casually.

But I pulled him in on to the grassy margin of the road, and we waited while the sound came ever closer. It was a motor-boat, sure enough, and it was coming in to Kilkieran quay below us. Soon the engine was switched off, and we guessed that the boat was drifting in to its moorings. I do not know how I guessed that that boat was something to be feared. We kept to the grass for the rest of the way, and stole into the shadow of the high fortress wall, whence we could look down at the boats. We picked out our own boat easily, gleaming whitely in the dark. Just beyond it we could make out the shape of another white boat, which we guessed to be the motor-boat. A figure carrying a lantern was standing on the quay wall, and as we watched it dropped on to the deck of the *Wave-Rider*.

"Someone boarding our boat!" said Joe in my ear.

"Perhaps it's one of the trawler-men," I said.

The lantern carrier opened our cabin door and flashed a brief light inside. Then he came out and looked about him, and at last climbed ashore again. We saw him move down the quay towards the fishing-boats. Then he bawled out:

"Hey, you! Where are the people that came in this boat?"

I felt a horrid sickness come over me. Joe grasped my arm till it hurt. It was Pat Conway.

A voice answered Pat at once, so that I knew the men on the fishing-boats had been watching him since he arrived. It was a slow voice, the voice of a man who has plenty of time to spare, who hopes for a little fun out of the stranger, and who does not like to be shouted at.

"What boat would you be talking about, Mister?"

"That white sailing-boat, of course."

"Oh, that white sailing-boat, is it? Ah, yes."

There was a pause, and we saw the fisherman's pipe reddening in the gloom, as he pulled at it peacefully.

"Come on, come on!" roared Pat. "Do you think I can

stand here all night? Tell me where did the people go off the boat!"

The fisherman laughed and made a remark in Irish to his listening companions.

"You're in a great hurry, Mister, to be sure," he said then. He called across to another boat. "Tomás! Did you see any people landing off that white boat?"

"What boat, Micil?" the voice came back, a slow, mocking voice.

"The white sailing-boat," said Micil. "Our friend here is in a great hurry to know."

"Now what would he want to know for?" said Tomás. "Is he the police?"

"Are you the police?" Micil asked Pat.

"I am not the police," said Pat with awful restraint.

"Maybe you'd be in the fishing, then," said Tomás.

"I am not in the fishing," said Pat, holding on to his temper with an effort. "I only asked you where did my friends go off the boat."

"Ah," said Micil, and pulled at his pipe again.

"Come on," I whispered to Joe. "We'll have to go down and pitch him a yarn before he comes looking for us. If I get Pat away, take the boat around to Bunraha, and I'll meet you there to-morrow night after dark."

We slipped out of the shadows and walked down the quay. Pat had now really lost his temper, and was calling out abuse to the fishermen. They made no answer, but I knew they would be holding their breath with delight as they listened. It was queer to think of all those grinning faces in the dark, and the odd sense of humour that had made them take this revenge on Pat for his rudeness.

As we came near him I called out:

"Mr. Conway!"

He stopped in the middle of a word. He came running towards us.

"Is that you, boy? Are you all right?" Then, as I expected, the short suspicious pause. "Where is Matt?" He caught me by the collar and shook me. "If you have done any harm to Matt, I'll slit your gizzard!"

Again Micil's mocking voice came from his boat.

"There's a nice friendly meeting!"

A rattle of laughter rose from the boats nearby. Pat dropped his hand. I said:

"Matt is sick. We had to take him to Kilbricken."

I felt a cold clamminess all over me as Pat said:

"Matt sick? I don't believe it. Matt is never sick."

"He didn't believe it himself," I said quickly, and I blushed in the dark at the ease with which the story rolled off my tongue. "We were just outside the lighthouse when he got out the brandy-bottle and began to drink out of it. He said he'd kill us if we took it from him. He was at the bottle for a long time, and then he went to sleep. When he woke up he was raving. He said little green men were hopping in and out of his pockets, and he kept trying to kill them with his knife. We were afraid he would hurt himself, so we took the knife from him. He was too weak to stop us."

I showed him Matt's knife, and for some reason this seemed to make him believe my story.

"That brandy-bottle," he muttered to himself. "Go on, boy."

"When we came near the island," I said, "he told us to land, and bring him to the doctor. We were going to land at Kilbricken, but he said that Kilkieran would be safer, and not to draw attention to ourselves. So we came in here, and we got him ashore in the dark, and helped him the two miles of the road to Kilbricken. We'd never have got there only for a man who gave us a lift on a cart."

"It's well I came after you," said Pat. "I got a feeling that something would go wrong, and I thought, if I saw you beyond Fort Island, you'd be safe enough after that."

Safe enough, in your way, thought I. Pat was rolling his chin in his hand to help him to think.

"I could go with you instead of Matt," he said, and my heart sank. "But then I would have to leave Matt here, and Matt has a long tongue. I hope he hasn't said too much already."

"I'm sure he has not," said Joe.

"Well, Michael, there's nothing for it but to go to the village and see him," said Pat.

"Joe can stay here and mind the boats," I said eagerly. "I wouldn't trust those fishermen," I added in a low tone.

So Joe went aboard the *Wave-Rider*, and sat by the helm looking as if he would not move until we came back. Gripping my elbow, Pat steered me up the quay and on to the dark road. I wished he would not hold me, for the feel of his hand on my arm sucked all the courage out of me. I tried to speak, but I could think of nothing to say. I wished that Kilbricken was forty miles away instead of two. Pat marched along so fast that I was afraid I would not be able to think of a way of ridding myself of his company before we would reach the village.

Soon we came to a desolate part of the road, where the low wind cried dismally among the rocks and the sea came in and out in pools by the roadside. Ahead of us, the lighthouse continually flashed its sabre across the night, making the road and the shore brilliant for a second before passing on.

In one of these flashes I saw a man walking on the grass by the roadside. He was dressed in blue homespun, like all the islanders, and he wore rawhide shoes, so that he moved without a sound. Pat had seen him too, and when we drew level, he said:

"A fine evening."

"A fine evening, indeed," said the man, "black enough for them that don't want to be seen."

"An honest man does not fear the light," said Pat heartily. "I'm going to Kilbricken to visit a sick friend."

"I wish I had a sick friend in Kilbricken," said the man. "I'm going there because I left my boat there, and I'm a man that does not like people to take too much notice of him."

"I wouldn't have spoken to you only that I thought it would shorten the road for the both of us," said Pat huffily.

"You're a very hasty man," said our strange companion. "You can talk to me, and welcome, for I think you don't like the light no more than myself, for all your sick friend in Kilbricken."

Now I noticed that he did not speak like the islanders. I wondered where he had got the clothes he wore.

"My name is Pat Conway," said Pat heatedly, "and I'm an honest boat-builder from the town."

"Ah!" The man let the word twang on the air like a violin string. "How strange! My name is Pat Conway too, and my profession is the same as yours!"

Pat's voice shook with rage.

"You are an ill-mannered lout," he shouted, "to insult an innocent stranger without cause!"

"Now, listen to me, Pat Conway," said the man in a low voice. "I am a dangerous man, because I am in danger. The police would be glad to know where I am, the gallant police in Kilbricken. Now do you see why I do not tell you my name and business, nor raise my voice even in a lonely place like this? If you are the cause of my arrest, I'll find you out sooner or later, and the people of these parts will have to learn to build their own boats. Do you understand me?"

In all my life I never heard such menace in such mild-sounding words. The man had an air of knowing one's thoughts, so that it seemed there would be no escape for whoever betrayed him. Pat was impressed at this threat.

"I understand you," he said. "I'll forget you as soon as we reach Kilbricken."

"You may begin to forget me now," said the man, "for I'm not going to walk with you to Kilbricken."

And in the next flash of light we saw him leap the low wall on to the shore, and that was the last we saw of him.

He had frightened Pat, and as we went along he held my arm still, but now he seemed to be looking for comfort from me. He told me he did not like the night and dark places, especially in strange country. He talked of ghosts and fairies until I found myself anxiously watching every landmark we passed for signs of evil activity. We were both relieved when we turned a corner and saw the lights of Kilbricken village curving round its own little bay.

It was a haphazard collection of houses, thrown anyhow on the hillside above the sea. Queer little laneways ran in and out among the houses, and gardens had been made on top of outcropping rocks here and there, so that cabbages waved above our heads as we walked on the road below. At one place there was a sort of little square, with a cross to commemorate the great famine of 1848. In that year, thousands of people died from want of food on the mainland, because the potato crop failed. But the famine never came to the islands, so they put up the cross for thanks.

Here among the houses there was shelter from the wind. At the foot of the cross a Spanish sailor was sitting, clear in the light that streamed from the open door of a public-house. He was singing a soft song of his own country, full of runs and trills, and looking upwards at the black sky. He took no notice of us when we paused in the shadow near him, and spoke in low voices.

"You had better go into the public-house and wait," I said, "while I go and speak to the doctor."

"You must take me for a fool," said Pat. "How do I know you won't disappear and never come back?"

This was just what I had planned to do, but I tried to look innocent as I said:

"Very well, then. Come along. But I warned the doctor to let no one see Matt. He may not let you in."

"He'll let me in, all right, when you tell him," said Pat curtly. "Lead on, please!"

I guessed from this that Pat did not know where the doctor lived, and I blessed my luck. I did not know what to do next, but I thought that if I could keep Pat busy without arousing his suspicions, Joe would have more time to get the boat away safely. What was to become of myself I dared not think.

I led him down along the water-front, and then at random through a lane that ended at a crossroads. In front was a long thatched house with a light showing. I could read "P. Kelly, Hotel," on the glass above the door. We tiptoed past the hotel, and past a closed shop, while my feeling of desperation increased. Then we came to the police barracks.

Two policemen were sitting on the steps outside, enjoying the night air. Their silver buttons shone in the light of an oil-lamp in the hallway behind them. They were big fellows, both. Suddenly I saw what to do.

I darted in front of Pat and grappled with him, while I shouted for help at the top of my voice. The two policemen rushed forward, and a third came running from the barracks. Doors began to open and people came out to watch until we were the centre of a little crowd.

"He's a thief, he's a robber!" I shouted, while Pat snarled threats at me.

"None of that, now!" said the biggest policeman, who wore a sergeant's stripes on his sleeve.

He seized Pat by the back of his collar, and turned him so that the dim light from the door fell on his face. Then he called excitedly:

"Ned! Come and look! It's Jimmy Folan—the one they call the Rat. Aha, my boy, we got your description and your picture from headquarters to-day! You're not very like the picture, but the description fits you fine. Come along, now." He turned to one of the others. "They said he was heading this way. This is a great capture."

I supposed that Jimmy Folan, the Rat, could have been our secretive acquaintance on the road from Kilkieran, and I prayed that he would get away safely.

The sergeant began to push Pat towards the open barrack door.

"Let me go!" shouted Pat. "I have to visit my sick friend. Let me go!"

The sergeant laughed heartily.

"A sick friend!" said he. "If you're who we think you are, your friend will have time to get better and come to visit you before you're about again."

They were simple people, those policemen, and there was not much crime in Fort Island. It never occurred to them that Pat might not be the criminal they were seeking. It was enough that he was a stranger. I hoped it would be morning before he would be able to convince them that he had done nothing against the law.

Since the policeman did not seem at all interested in me, I slipped in among the crowd and away. Soon I came to the cross again, where the Spaniard was still singing. And then I turned up the hill away from the sea, on my way to meet Joe at Bunraha.

★ IX ★

Bunraha was the name of the village at the farthest tip of the island, as I had learned from our map. The map showed only one road. This bisected the island from end to end, running up over the ridge and down into the plain at the far side, up again, and at last down a precipitous slope to the sea.

I knew that Fort Island was covered with a network of byroads, but Joe had warned me not to trust to them. Some of them ran into the sea, others ended in cliffs or unscaleable rocks, and all of them were pitted with dangerous holes. Only the islanders understood the vagaries of those roads. I decided to keep to the main road, although I would have to be careful to keep out of sight. I thought that this would not be too difficult, for it was late now, and the lights in the cottages were going out one by one.

I kept in the shadow of the low stone wall and walked up the hill for about a mile. Then I came to a line of cottages whose doors and windows opened directly on to the road. They were all in darkness, and as I tiptoed past I heard a mighty snore from one of them. It was the snore of a man who works at his sleep, who values every moment of it. Suddenly I felt the accumulated weariness of the whole day settle down on my shoulders. With all my heart I envied that snorer his good bed and his good supper. For I was wildly hungry too, though I had had no time to think of it until now.

Beyond the cottages I paused. It was no use trying to go on, for my stomach and my legs were my enemies. It seemed that I would have to sleep and eat, or I would be so weak that I would surely fall into Pat Conway's hands again.

A little away from the last cottage, on the opposite side of the road, I could make out a building in the dimness. I found that it was an old shed, with a roof made of sods with the grass still growing on them. A broken door hung sideways at the entrance. I went in, and found it dry and warm inside. It was used for storing turf, and a pile of old mould against the wall would make as soft a bed as anyone could wish for.

But first I must find something to eat. There were a few hens snuggled warmly in the turf-mould, but when I lifted them one by one, I found that they had not a single egg to show between them all. They swore softly at me and settled down again.

I went out of the shed and stole round to the back of the cottages. And there on the window-sill I found a meal fit for a king. It was a flat basket of sally rods, full of cooked potato-peelings, for the hens' breakfast. There was even a potato or two buried deep among them, as I could feel. A little glow was coming now from the hidden moon, or I should never have found them. I carried the basket bodily away to my shed, and sat like a lord feasting among the contemptuous hens. Someone had strained tea-leaves through the basket, but I was too hungry to care for that.

I had no sooner made my meal than I stretched out on the turf-mould and slept like one dead. It was the soft cluck of the hens that woke me. A bar of sunlight was coming in through a crack in the old door. Grains of dust danced madly in it, kicked up by the scratching feet of the hens. I was hungry again, but the remains of last night's meal repelled me now. It was well the dark had hidden it.

I listened at the door for sounds of movement, but there were none. I slipped outside, and without one backward glance, I raced along the road away from my night's lodging.

I judged that it was about six o'clock, for the sun was still low. Soon the people would be about their work, and it would be very hard to escape attention. If I was to have breakfast, it must be soon.

Then I saw a house standing by itself in a field. There was no gateway—only a stile made of the stone of the wall. The door of the house stood open and a feather of smoke came from the chimney. I climbed boldly over the wall, and went to the door and looked in.

A man was bent double at the hearth, fanning the spark of a fire to flame with his cap. A kettle of water hung on the crane over the fire.

"God save all here," I said.

He turned slowly to look at me, while he went on fanning. He was a man of about fifty. His hair was cut close, except for a tuft in front, left there to be seen when he wore his cap. When he settled the cap on his head again, I could see that it was as much a part of him as his hair. He had deep brown eyes, as round as an otter's and with the same perpetual mild surprise in them. His voice was soft and deep too.

"Come in, boy, come in," he said. "You're about very early."

I stepped into the kitchen. The table was laid with a flowery mug, a knife and a huge cake of soda-bread, like a cart-wheel. There was one plate on the dresser, and one chair at the table. It did not need much insight to see that he lived alone.

"I was going to wet the tea, if that kettle would boil," he said. "Had you your breakfast?"

I said no, that I was out too early. Though he knew that I was a stranger on the island, he did not ask me any questions. He set me to cut slices from the big soda-cake for both of us, and then he brought a pat of yellow butter from the dresser. He made the tea, and courteously gave me the mug, while he drank from a saucer.

"That's my own butter," he said. "I make it as well as any woman."

I praised the butter, and he looked pleased and told me that he made the bread himself too. He had a married sister in the town, who was always wanting to send her daughter to housekeep for him.

" 'Poor Patcheen' she calls me," he said with a grin, "but I said that poor Patcheen is getting on all right by himself. Maybe you know her, a big tall thin woman, married to a man called Conneeley with an eating-house on the potato-market."

I said that I did not know his sister, and he made me promise to go and see her when I would get home.

"Once she left the island, she never came back," he said. "But now I think she'd like one of her daughters to marry an islander, the way she'd have an excuse for coming here sometimes."

When we had finished our meal I thanked him.

"You're welcome," was all he said, and he did not even watch me down the field to the road.

I was glad to have chanced on a host who took so little interest in other people's affairs.

Before all the doors began to open, I had time to go down the hill to the narrowest part of the island. Here was still another quay, and a village called Kilbenen on a side road. I had got bolder now that I was more than halfway to Bunraha, and I even whistled as I walked up the next hill. But a few minutes later I got a fright that set my heart thundering, and again brought me up sharp against the dangers I was in.

I had just reached an old cemetery about half a mile beyond Kilbenen. The gravestones were set haphazard among the ruins of an old monastery, and docks and nettles grew wild everywhere. I paused to rest with my elbows on the wall, and to dream about the monks who have lived here once so long ago. I could see downhill to where the sea gleamed with blue fire a mile away, and the clop-clop of a horse's hooves on the road only made the stillness seem deeper.

Suddenly I shook myself out of my dream. The horse was coming towards me from the direction of Kilbricken. It was still hidden by the bend of the road, but I could hear metal-bound wheels bumping over the stones and crunching the sand as they bowled along. I knew it must be a side-car. There were no other carts on the island that could move as fast as that.

I flashed over the wall, among the nettles. They stung me cruelly, but I had no time for them. I found a chink in the wall to look through.

It was a side-car all right. An islander was on the box, flicking his whip over the big chestnut horse's back. And on either side, glaring ahead as if they would make short work of anyone who got in their way, were Pat Conway and his friend, Matt.

I dropped back among the nettles, sick with fright, and panting at the thought of my narrow escape. I had half hoped that the police would keep Pat for a few days, perhaps until the next boat would come from the mainland. By then Joe and I would be safe on the high seas. But now it seemed that he must have proved quite soon that he was not the Rat Folan. Else how had he had time to go back to Kilkieran and release Matt, and be so hot on my trail so early in the morning?

The question that disturbed me most was how he had found out where I had gone. I did not doubt for a moment that he was pursuing me. Perhaps the woman who missed the hens' breakfast had raised the hue and cry. Or perhaps Patcheen, who had looked so uninterested, had lost no time in telling everyone about his early guest. Somehow it hurt me to think of this.

It was obvious now that I must leave the main road. Bunraha must still be my goal, since Joe would look for me there. But there was no hope now of getting there before Pat and Matt. I hoped that Joe would keep the boat outside until nightfall, when she would have some chance of slipping in to the quay unnoticed.

Down by the cemetery, a road ran towards the sea. I climbed the stile and came out on to it. Now I had time to feel the pain from the nettle-stings, and I bound dock-leaves around the blisters to ease them. It was well on in the morning by now, and from every cottage door someone peered to watch me pass. I tried to look as if I were in no hurry, climbing walls and walking along the top, sending stones spinning down the road and playing all the aimless tricks of a boy who is out for a sunny day's enjoyment. I never paused long enough for anyone to question me. When the fat, curious old women began to waddle towards me, I ran and skipped down the road so fast that they could never have caught me.

Presently the road came out on to the shore. There were no houses here, for the Atlantic storms tore in all winter, lifting giant rocks and rolling the heavy stones about like marbles. No house could have survived these storms. I was able to go much faster now that no one was watching. The road ran along the top of the shore. It was not a real road, but the stones had been flattened down by the carts which came in spring and summer to draw home seaweed for manure. I followed it till it ended in huge black barnacle-covered rocks, and then another road led inland, uphill again.

Soon the houses began again. They were smaller and poorer now, for this land was the worst in the whole island. I climbed to the top of the hill, and looked away down to the westward, where the road led. And down there I could see the white houses and the little quay of Bunraha.

There was a tall white lighthouse there, on a little island about a quarter of a mile out from the shore. It had its own little pier, and a couple of grey stone cottages crouching at its foot. The pier was painted white, and the long wall to one side of it. It made a pretty picture, with the clear blue sea stretching away and away behind it.

As I came down the grass-grown road to the village, I saw the new tracks made by the side-car. The narrow iron bands on the wheels had left clear straight lines. In the middle of the road drifting sand had lodged, and it held the prints of the horse's hooves. The hill was so steep that the backs of his shoes had made deeper marks as he had gone cautiously downwards. A few moments later I turned the corner, and there, a few yards away, was the side-car itself.

I shrank back at once, and then looked out again more cautiously. The side-car stood at the open door of a house which had an advertisement for Guinness's stout outside. This was the public-house, it seemed, and it was the only two-storied house in Bunraha.

A big bush grew by the door, and I slipped across and pressed into it. From there the voices inside came to me with extraordinary clearness. I shuddered a little as Pat's laugh boomed out through the doorway. If he came out now, I was lost.

Soon I guessed that he was drinking comfortably inside, and I leaned towards the door to listen. A woman's voice was answering his last question.

"That's all I know, sir. No strange boy came here at all this morning. Sure, don't I know every boy on the island?"

"Maybe he came without you seeing him," said Pat.

The woman snorted.

"No one could do that," she said. "And to prove it I'll tell you I've heard something about that boy already."

"What did you hear? Come on, woman, what did you hear?"

Pat spoke roughly in his excitement.

"Easy on," said the woman, and she sounded quite offended. "I was going to tell you if you'd have patience. There was a strange boy on the road from Kilbricken, for he had breakfast with Patcheen Phaddy at the crack of dawn this morning."

"Do you hear that, Matt? Where does this Patcheen live?"

"A mile the other side of Kilbenen," said the woman. "Halfways and more between here and Kilbricken."

"Then we're on the right track," said Pat triumphantly. "There's not much you don't know, ma'am, for sure."

"Patcheen Phaddy isn't half curious enough," said the woman. "He never asked him what brought him to the island, nor where he was going at that hour of the morning. It was only by chance he mentioned to someone that went in, that the boy had been there at all."

By the note of wonder in her voice it was clear that she did not understand Patcheen's kind of mind.

Next I could imagine her leaning her elbows confidentially on the counter as she said:

"And what would you be wanting with this boy, anyway?"

"To cut his heart out!" said Matt in a savage growl.

"God bless my soul!" said the woman. "And what has the poor boy done to you?"

"That's only Matt's little joke," said Pat. "Isn't that so, Matt?"

Matt growled again, not at all like one who jokes.

"We're afraid the boy is wandering in his mind," said Pat easily. "His mother asked us to find him and bring him home. He left home a few days ago in a boat he stole from me. Not that I mind that, of course. I know he means no harm. I'm more concerned about himself than about the old boat. Now, if you should see him, ma'am, just get him into a room quietly, like, and lock the door on him. That's the best thing to do. Then send for me, and I'll take him home to his mother."

"You black-hearted scoundrel!" said I under my breath, in the bush.

"Is he dangerous?" the woman asked, breathlessly.

"A little, only a little," said Pat. "He gave me the slip last night, though. And he played a nice trick on me too. He told the police in Kilbricken that I was a criminal, ha-ha, what do you think of that?"

Again Matt growled like a savage beast. Pat went on hastily, so as to cover this up:

"I don't mind that at all. I'm only for his good. But if you'll help me to capture him, ma'am, you'll be doing him a good turn, and his mother will be very thankful to you."

There was a sound of chair-legs scraping on the floor as he went on.

"I'd like to leave the old side-car here while we go over to visit the light-keepers. We won't be too long, and you can hold the boy here in talk, maybe, if you can't lock him up."

They were making for the door now.

"You'll have another little drink, sir, just one small one for luck before you go."

That last drink saved me. While Pat was praising her hospitality, and Matt was presumably lapping up the liquor, I slipped out of the bush, round to the back of the house, and into the only shed that was there.

It turned out to be a hen-house. This was the second time in twelve hours that I had found refuge among hens. There were one or two sitting on their nests, and they clucked at me in an irritated way. Then they settled down again and fixed beady fierce eyes on me. I stood as still as I could, and hoped they would forget about me.

Presently I heard Pat's voice calling farewells to the woman in the shop, and then the sound of their feet died away on the gravel.

I held my breath and listened. About me there were the other houses of the village, with people who would surely see me if I tried to slip away. I did not want to spend the day among the hens. Indeed I had conceived a deep dislike of hens in the last few hours.

The next thing that happened was something that I had not foreseen at all. As I stood leaning against the hen-house wall, I heard feet approaching. I got quickly behind the door, prepared to fight my way out, if need be. I thought it might be well to surprise the newcomer, whoever it might be. The only weapon I could find was a short lath which had once been part of a nesting-box. Armed with this, I waited for the door to open.

The footsteps paused outside. The door was flung open, and a shaft of light flew in. I raised my lath—and then I dropped it on the floor.

For a gently humorous voice, the voice of the woman I had heard talking to Pat and Matt, said softly:

"You can come out now, young lad. They're gone away."

"Are you going to try to lock me up?" I whispered fiercely. "It would be safer not to try."

"Tut-tut!" said she. "I wouldn't think of such a thing. Slip out now, quick. There's no one looking."

I decided to trust her. She did not sound like a person who would betray me without hearing my version of the story.

I stepped out into the sunshine, and the woman and I looked each other over. She was small, but very fat and wide. Her hair was red with a streak of grey, and her piercing blue eyes danced with interest in all that happened around her.

"You don't look very dangerous," she said. "Come in this way."

As she led me in by the back door to the house, I said:

"I'm not wandering in my mind, either."

"Neither am I," said she drily. "They must have thought I was, to believe their yarn."

She brought me into her kitchen and made me sit down at the table.

"How did you know I was in the hen-house?" I asked.

"I heard the hens clucking," she said. "They never do that at this time of the day. I knew you were in the bush by the door before that. I delayed the men with a free drink, though I grudged them sore, to give you time to get away."

"You seem to know everything," I said.

"Oh, I take an interest. I'm curious, some people say. But curiosity is not always such a bad thing. If you know all the queer things that are happening, you can do something to stop them."

She peeped out of the door into the shop. Then she closed the door carefully and came back to the fire.

"Now I'm going to get a meal," she said. "And while I'm getting it you can be telling me the whole story. Oh, don't fear anyone will hear you," as she noticed my glance at the door. "No one from the village ever comes in at this time, and if our two friends come back I'll have plenty of time to hide you."

So I began at the beginning and told her the whole story. It was clear that I needed her help, and the price of her help was my story. Once or twice I tried to take a short cut but she brought me back each time and made me fill in the parts I had left out. Long before I had done, she had given up her preparations for my meal and was sitting before me at the table with her eyes fixed on my face and her lips parted as she followed the tale.

At last I finished. She sighed deeply and dropped her hands into her lap.

"Well, you're a queer pair of heroes, there's no doubt," she said. "It's Pat Conway that's dangerous, and I can see that I'll have to help you."

"If you help me they may injure you," I said, for I thought it would be wrong not to warn her.

"Just let them try, that's all!"

She got up briskly and took the kettle off the fire. As she made the tea, she said:

"I'm going to have a cup with you, for I'm as tired from listening to your story as if I had been hopping along with you since you left home."

She boiled two brown eggs for me, and as we sat there eating, I savoured the moment of peace.

Too soon we were finished.

"You can't stay here in the kitchen," she said, "in case our two friends come back. But I have a fine feather bed upstairs, softer than any heap of turf-mould, and you can spend the day there. You may not sleep as soft again for a long time."

"But Pat may search the house."

"If he puts his foot beyond the kitchen door, I'll yell blue murder," she said with a grin. "Then the neighbours will all come and throw the pair of them into the tide. Anyway I don't expect them back for a while. When I heard they were friends of the light-keepers, I knew what to think of them."

I was very much surprised at this. She told me that the pair of light-keepers at Bunraha were a blot on the fair name of the light-keepers of Ireland. She hinted at dark deeds, and wild nights of carousing on the ill-gotten gains.

"But how am I going to get away?" I asked. "Joe will bring the boat around here to-night, and I must be able to meet him."

"I've thought of that," she said. "The light-keepers have several boats, and they always keep one below here at the quay. You must take that boat. I'll show you where to get the oars. You must wait for the dark, of course. Then you can row around to a cave that I know about, that can only be reached from the sea, and you can watch out for Joe from there. There will be a moon to-night, I'm thinking, by the look of the weather."

"I think you know everything in the world," I said.

She led me upstairs then, and showed me where I was to sleep. Then she left me, and I could hear her pattering off downstairs.

I went to look out of the window, and found that I could see the lighthouse on its island, held in a blue haze of heat. I watched for a while, but I could see no sign of movement there. A row-boat tied up at the quay rose and fell on the swell, and that was all. I took off my coat and lay down on the bed. It was indeed much softer than the turf-mould, and in spite of my danger I soon fell asleep.

Hours later, in the grey hollow between sleeping and waking, I heard hooves, and the grinding of wheels on sand. I sat up to listen and heard the sounds die away. A few minutes after that there was a soft tap on the door, and the red-haired woman came in.

"They're gone back towards Kilbricken," she said. "You'd better get away at once, for they may hear news of you at any moment. Then they'll come back hot foot, you may be sure."

I sprang up, asking:

"What time is it?"

"It's five o'clock," she said. "It won't be dark for a few hours, but you must get away at once all the same."

"But the light-keepers will see me."

"I've attended to that," she said. "I've sent Big Johnny Conneeley over with a present of whiskey, and he'll keep them occupied until you get away."

"And the people in the village?"

"They'll mind their own business. They have no reason to love the light-keepers. Big Johnny's son, Mike, is going to go round to the cave with you, in his currach. Big Johnny does what I tell him."

She had said she would help me, but all this kindness was more than anyone could have hoped for. She told me her name was Sally Rua MacDonagh—red-haired Sally.

"There is one thing Big Johnny would not do for me," she went on. "I asked him to go with you to find your island, but he would not. He said that's an unlucky island, that any man that ever saw it never had a day's luck after."

"Then the people here know about the island?" I said eagerly.

"They do, but they won't talk about it. There have been too many wrecks there, they say. But I know that's all nonsense. You'll get there safely, and you'll come and visit me here on your way home."

I promised to do that, though I wondered if I would ever set foot on Fort Island again. She had a parcel of eggs ready for me downstairs, and a loaf of bread. Then she led me out by the back way, and we started down to the quay.

★ X ★

The next part of the story concerns Joe.

When Pat and I had started on the road to Kilbricken, he sat there for a long time waiting for a quiet moment to slip away. At last, one by one, the men began to haul up the heavy sails of their hookers, to go out for a night's fishing. There was not much light, but Joe knew what they were doing, because they called to each other across the water as they made ready. Quietly he began to get the *Wave-Rider's* mainsail up.

Though he was sure the men saw this, not one of them spoke. He was able to hurry then, for he guessed that no one would try to hinder him. Still it was slow work, for she was a big boat for one boy to handle. At last he slipped his moorings and stood out into the harbour.

Just then he heard approaching feet clattering and a voice shouting. It was Matt, escaped somehow from his prison. Joe made for the harbour-mouth. Matt saw the boat's white gleam in the dimness and shrieked to him to stop. He called to the men in the boats to block his way.

"And why would we do that?" came Micil's voice.

"He's a thief! He's stealing the boat! Catch him!"

"Do you tell me that, now?" said Micil, in mock astonishment. "Did you ever hear the like of that for wickedness?"

"Get after him, you cawbogue!" roared Matt, dancing with rage on the quay.

Micil settled down to enjoy himself.

"Tomás!" he called to his friend. "Come up out of that till you see the wee man dancing the Rinnce Fada all by himself!"

Tomás came up out of the hold of his own boat, and so did all the other men who had not gone off to the fishing grounds. Like all the Fort Islanders, they loved to see a mainlander looking foolish. They told Matt in maddening detail that they never got caught up in other people's quarrels.

"We don't even know whether the boy stole the boat from you, or you are trying to steal the boat from the boy," said Micil.

And he quoted a number of complicated Irish proverbs to prove that his ancestors would have agreed with him.

Long before he had finished, Joe had his boat sailing out of the harbour and round the point towards Bunraha. Away out to sea, he could see the little lights of the fishing-boats. On the island there were the cottage lights to guide him. He kept far out, for fear of reefs and submerged rocks, for he did not know the coast of Fort Island very well. He was afraid to show a light to read his map, lest Matt were already on his trail. The dull glow of the moon through the clouds made it possible for him to see the outlines of the island, and he had to make the most of that.

There was only a light breeze now, and he did not make much headway. While I was sleeping comfortably among the hens, he was moving ever so slowly before the breeze, and wondering if before dawn came he would reach a safe anchorage in which to spend the day. He passed the village called Cronagaorach, which means the Sheepfold, just before dawn, and then he came to the high sheer cliffs below the Fort.

Where the cliffs curved inward he hove to, and lowered his sails. The first light came and found him in a clear, deep, natural harbour, screened on all sides from the land. Surely, he thought, no one would climb out to the very cliff edge to see him. He could be seen from the sea, of course, but he must trust to luck there. Another serious danger was that if a storm rose, the boat would certainly be dashed to pieces against the cliffs. In winter storms, the spray from the gigantic waves often rose above the cliff-tops and was blown across the whole island. Even now, a white line of surf gnashed its teeth against the rock behind him.

He cast his anchor, and watched it weave its way through the clear green water to the bottom, where it held firmly. Then he cooked a meal and ate it, and lay down in the cabin to sleep uneasily. Every hour he got up to see that the anchor was secure, that he was not observed from the sea, or that the day had not slipped away while he slept. It was the longest day of his life, he said.

Meanwhile, as we pieced the story together later, Matt had given up his war-dance on the quay. With a final round of abuse at the placid Micil and Tomás and their friends, he stumped off towards the road to Kilbricken. The fishermen spent a happy ten minutes mimicking his actions with shrieks of laughter. Then they turned their minds to serious business, and sailed off to their fishing.

Matt fairly burned up the road to Kilbricken, as the saying is. He had no idea where to look for Pat. He questioned the singing Spanish sailor, and only got a long stare and a run of impassioned grace-notes for an answer. He went into the public-house opposite the cross, but a long-necked man was standing on top of a barrel facing the crowd, and had just begun to sing:

Come all ye true-born Irishmen, and listen to my song.
It's only forty verses, so I won't detain you long.
'Tis all about . . .

Matt slipped out again. He had learned a little wisdom in the last hour or two, and he was no longer willing to provide fun for the islanders.

At last, it was a boy he found standing in a dark doorway who told him that Pat had been captured by the police. He found his way to the little barrack.

The door was shut now, but he could see Pat through the uncurtained window. He was sitting at a table in the day-room, being guarded by the big sergeant, who looked like a sheep-dog who has cornered a particularly troublesome sheep. Matt was not quite satisfied with his view of the room. He stepped into the flower-bed under the window, to peer through the glass. A moment later he heard a howl of rage behind him, and a heavy hand grasped him by the collar. With his head held down, all he could see was furious blue legs and silver buttons as he was marched into the day-room.

"This rat, this—thing—standing among my wallflowers—" his captor spluttered to the sergeant.

Pat had started to his feet.

"That's my sick friend you have there. Where did you find him?"

"I found him trampling down my wallflowers that I reared from the seeds." He turned to the sergeant, pleading. "Just let me give him one clout, one little paste that will crack his jaw-bone and teach him to respect people's wallflowers!"

"Easy now, Ned," said the sergeant. "So this is your sick friend," he said to Pat.

"He'll be a very sick friend when I'm finished with him," growled Ned.

The sergeant took Matt out of Ned's hands like a hunter taking a wild duck from a red setter. Then he made Ned stand on guard by the door, and sat down himself behind the table.

"Now, what's all this about?" he said sternly. "What do you mean by going around impersonating the Rat Folan, wasting the country's time? You're no more the Rat than I am."

"How do you know that?" asked Pat, with creditable patience.

"Because the Rat always travels alone, of course. So you can give up pretending to be the Rat, and tell me what you're really up to, or I'll have you in Court for obstructing the Law!"

"I'm not the Rat," said Pat bitterly. "I'm a respectable businessman from the town. That boy who was the cause of my arrest stole my boat and now, thanks to you, he has probably got away with it."

But the Sergeant was not as foolish as all that. He wanted to know why, if I had stolen the boat, Pat had not informed the police in the town. He had not even informed the police on the island. An honest man, said the Sergeant, does not try to administer justice himself. He calls in the Law to his aid. It was in the Book.

The Sergeant reached behind him and took a book off the mantelshelf. He thumbed it back and forth until he found the place, and then read the piece aloud.

Now, Pat, above all things, did not want the police to find me and Joe. He guessed that if we were questioned we would probably mention that Matt had threatened our lives, and that Pat, by trying to get back his boat, was breaking his contract with us. So he tried to make the sergeant believe that he had decided to drop the whole affair.

The sergeant did not believe him. Ned said that a man who walks on wallflowers is a thief and a murderer. They ended, however, by letting both of them go, for they could think of no good excuse for holding them.

Pat and Matt came out of the barracks quietly. They

were surprised at being freed so easily, and they feared that they might be hauled back again at any moment. They went down to the quays and looked for a man to drive them to Bunraha.

"But we're just going to bed," said the men with the side-cars. "It's nearly midnight."

"I'll pay you well," said Pat.

But they all said money was not everything, and a good night's sleep was to be valued above the gold of princes.

"And what would be taking you to Bunraha at this hour of the night?" they wanted to know.

"To visit the light-keepers," said Pat.

They explained to him that if the light-keepers were the right kind of people, they would be in their beds long before a side-car could reach Bunraha. On the other hand, if they were out of bed, it would prove that they were bad kind of people, and it would not be safe for a decent gentleman like Pat to go to visit them. They assured him that light-keepers have to sleep like ordinary people, and they offered to show him their own light-keeper in his bed at that very moment, to prove it. They were enjoying themselves thoroughly. Pat saw it was no use arguing with them. He engaged one of them to drive to Bunraha in the morning, but he could not persuade him to start early.

"What's all the hurry about?" said the driver. "Your friends won't get away."

So Pat and Matt had to spend the night in lodgings in Kilbricken. It was no wonder that when they passed me at the cemetery beyond Kilbenen, their faces were still twisted with rage at the delay.

And all day, while Joe slept on the boat and I at Sally Rua's house, they had plenty of time to plot our downfall.

The long slow fingers of dark were moving in over the water and the *Wave-Rider* was in deep shadow under the Fort before Joe began to make ready to leave his anchorage. He made another meal, of the cold remains of his morning one. Inside his little shelter it was calm, but he could see that outside there was enough wind to help him on his way. Still he waited, until the light was almost gone, and at last he hauled up his dripping anchor, and moved out to sea.

If he had looked upwards he might have seen a figure on the clifftops waving its arm as a signal to someone far below.

An hour or two before Joe sailed, I was at the quay at Bunraha, where Sally Rua had led me in the late afternoon. An island boy was sitting there, waiting for us. He was Big Johnny Conneeley's son, Mike. He was shy, like all the island boys, but he had a wild eye, and he twitched his bare toes nervously on the warm stones as we approached.

There was no one else in sight, but Sally spoke in a low voice.

"Have you the currach ready?"

"Yes, ma'am," said Mike.

He skipped down the stone steps to where the currach was tied to a ring. They are as light as a feather, these currachs, and they ride over the top of the water like gulls. They are made of canvas stretched over a lath frame and tarred, and they are the only safe small boats in the uneasy seas around the islands.

I stepped into the currach. There were only two seats for the oarsmen. Sally told me to sit on the floor in the stern, where I could not be seen. Then before I could thank her or say good-bye, she had slipped open the knot on the rope and pushed the boat away from the quay. Then she turned round and marched away without once looking back.

Mike grinned at me shyly.

"She said it would be better for me to take you to the

cave, since you don't know how to row. I'll show you how, when we get out a piece."

When we would get to the cave, he was to go off, leaving me the boat. When I would see Joe coming, I was to row out to meet him. Thus there would be no need for him to sail in to Bunraha quay, where he might be seen by the light-keepers. Then we could be off to our island without any more delay.

"I wish I could go with you," said Mike longingly. "I often heard Big Johnny talking about Inishmanann, but I'd be afraid to ask him to let me go."

"But what will I do with the currach?" I asked.

I knew the currachs were valued highly by the islanders, for a great deal of work went to the making of them.

"Let her drift," said Mike. "I'll be watching out for her, and I know exactly where she'll drift to—in on the reefs by Cronagaorach, where all the wrack comes in."

When we were half a mile out from the shore, he gave me a short lesson on rowing the currach. The oars were light and long and they had no blade. He showed me how to set the bows against a wave, and warned me above all against making any sudden movement. It was the easiest thing in the world to overturn a currach, he said. I had to learn quickly, because there was great risk of being seen from the shore if I stayed too long in sight. I comforted myself with the reflection that I would not have to row far.

Presently I was back on the floor, and then Mike turned the currach's nose in towards the shore again. In a few minutes we touched softly on shingle.

Mike shipped his oars quickly and hopped out into the water. He pulled the currach up on to a little round beach of gravel and stones. Sheer cliffs rose at the back of it, except where the dark mouth of a cave broke the surface at one place.

"You can stay in the cave and you won't be seen," Mike explained. "Fishing-boats may pass by, and you'll be needing cover. Shove off the currach carefully—you'd want to lift her bows as you push her stern into the water. A sharp stone would rip a hole in her in a second."

While he spoke, he was buttoning up his jacket.

"I'll be off now," he said. "I hope you won't have long to wait."

I was puzzled to know how he was going to leave the place. As far as I could see the only way there was from the sea.

Then Mike said:

"Here goes!"

And he simply climbed up the face of that cliff. My heart was in my mouth as I watched him. He moved from foothold to foothold like a fly. He never wavered for an instant, and he paused only once to beat off a flapping, squawking gull whose nest he had disturbed. At last he got to the top, where he hauled himself up on his stomach, and I saw him no more.

I let out a long sigh. Every moment I had expected him to come crashing down on to the beach at my feet. But now I realized that he must often have made that journey before. He had gone up the cliff as serenely as I had been accustomed to walk up the ladder to my own bedroom loft at home.

I went into the cave. It was not large, but the air in there was cold. I sat near the entrance on a flat stone, and settled down to watch for the *Wave-Rider*. As I waited I thought of my mother at home, thinking, to be sure, that we were well on our way to the island now, under the protection of Matt. It was well that she could not see me as I was, I thought grimly.

Presently the light began to go. I got uneasy lest Joe might wait until the pitch dark before venturing in to

Bunraha. Then I reflected that he would know I would be on the watch for him, and he would surely sail in with enough light for me to see him by. From where I sat I could see only a short stretch of sea, for the cliff blocked my view on the right-hand side, and a long arm of reef stretched out on the left, where Bunraha was.

Then, as I watched, a row-boat came into view coming from Bunraha. It was a wooden boat, I noticed, and it seemed to have only one occupant. My heart jumped as I realized that it must be one of the light-keepers. The boat was surely one of the heavy unwieldy ones that they used to ferry themselves to and from Bunraha. Sally Rua had told me that these were the only boats they had.

The man in the boat was behaving queerly. He had stopped rowing, and his boat was bobbing up and down just outside the reef, not fifty yards away from me. As I watched he shipped his oars. Then he took some string from his pocket and tied it on to one of the oars around the top. Then he dropped the oar into the water and let it trail at the end of the string, some distance away.

I was puzzled by this manoeuvre. Now he seemed to be just sitting there. I wondered if this were some strange method of fishing. I heartily wished he would go and fish somewhere else, for his presence there looked like spoiling our plan. And there came Joe, in the *Wave-Rider*, sailing along before the breeze.

After that everything happened quickly. The man in the boat hailed Joe. Joe hove to. The man manoeuvred his boat up to the *Wave-Rider* with one oar. He pointed to the other oar, floating in the water. Joe came to the side to look. He hesitated. Then he seemed to make up his mind. He threw a line to the man, who lost no time in hauling his own boat alongside the *Wave-Rider*. The man clambered on board. Then, while I watched with my silly mouth open, he lashed out at Joe and knocked him senseless. Then he rubbed his hand on his trousers and quietly began to sail the *Wave-Rider*, trailing his own boat, back to Bunraha.

My first instinct, when I came to, was to rush down to the shore screaming. I paused in time. The light-keeper need only come in and collect me, for I would not be able to climb the cliff face, and add my body to Joe's on the floor of our boat. He was not like Matt. The punch that had knocked out Joe had been a certain one. It was obviously not the first time the man had used his fists.

Now I was glad of the growing dark. As the *Wave-Rider* pulled out of sight, I launched the currach and set out to follow it at a safe distance. I was unhandy at the oars at first, of course, but by remembering Mike's advice I soon began to manage them better. Still, I was very slow, and by the time I rounded the reef the sailing-boat was out of sight.

I guessed that the man would take Joe straight to the lighthouse. They would be safe from interruption there, and the light-keepers did not seem to have any friends in Bunraha. So while night fell about me, I rowed for the lighthouse island as best I could.

I will not easily forget that journey. Since I had never rowed before, I soon had pains in my back and arms. My hands were raw too, from gripping the oars, but I dared not pause for a rest. But worst of all, I was so bad at managing the boat that all caution was out of the question. I could only make straight for the quay and pull in alongside the *Wave-Rider*, already moored there.

I was so tired now that I would not have protested if a rope had been thrown around me and I had been led ashore like a calf. I sat there in the boat, quite unable to move. The moon rode high through clouds, and gave me enough light to see about me. Still no one leaped on me. I stretched my arms and felt the cramp lessening. I had tried to come in quietly, but it seemed impossible that no one had heard me.

I stood up in the currach and climbed aboard the *Wave-Rider*. She was empty. Joe was gone. I went into the cabin, but though I had no light I could feel that there was no one there. For one wild moment I thought of trying to sail her away by myself, but I knew that to attempt it would be madness. Since a currach was too much for me, it was unlikely that I would be able for a sailing-boat.

Then I heard soft quick steps approaching. In a panic, I ducked into the cabin. The steps paused. Feet thudded on to the deck and the boat rocked from side to side. Light feet crossed to look over the side, at my currach, of course. Then a voice hissed:

"Michael!"

I peered out of the cabin, and felt a rush of relief. It was Mike Conneeley, Big Johnny's son. I came out of the cabin.

"What are you doing here? Where's Joe?"

"They left me to guard the boat," he said. "They took Joe up to the lighthouse."

"You guarding the boat!"

"After I left you, somehow I didn't want to go home. I saw Joe being captured. I was on top of the cliff. Then I came round to Bunraha and got a currach, and came over to the lighthouse. I was waiting on the quay here, all innocent, like, when the boat came in. The men know me on account of Big Johnny being my father, and they think I'm a friend of theirs. A fat fellow and a small ratty fellow came down to the quay to meet the boat too."

"That would be Pat Conway and Matt," I said. "They didn't go far on the road to Kilbricken."

"Yes, they called them Pat and Matt. They were all very pleased at having captured Joe. It seems they saw his boat anchored under the cliff quite early in the day, but they decided not to try to capture him there. That's never their way. And they have no good boats—only wooden row-boats. They knew you'd be planning to meet each other and they hoped they would get the two of you together. They didn't know you were at the cave—Big Johnny saw to that—but they guessed that you would come looking for Joe at the lighthouse."

"So they left you to guard the boat and tell them when I would come. It's lucky they picked on you."

"And now I heard them say that one of the light-keepers is going to go along with Matt to take charge of the two of you on the way to the island. They said it would take two to sail the boat home. They're planning to leave you behind on the island. I went up just now to listen at the window, and I heard their talk."

I was rather surprised that they still planned to bring us to the island, until I remembered that it would be a very convenient place to get rid of us. If they tried to dispose of us here, people might ask awkward questions. And to be sure, we would be useful to them on the voyage out.

"When do they plan to go?"

"Quite soon," said Mike. "They're putting things together now. They're only waiting for you to arrive."

"Then we must get Joe free at once. Where did they put him?"

"In a place where they thought no one would look. He's in the tower with the light."

"Is the door locked?"

"Yes, but we can break in easily. It's only a padlock. Have you any tools on the boat?"

We had a screwdriver in our toolbox, and Mike took this because he said it would be the quietest. He would unscrew the hasp of the padlock from the door-jamb, and we would not have to break the padlock at all.

"I'll turn loose my own currach before we go," he said.

"We may have to sail off in a hurry. My father will find it in the morning."

"But how will you get home? We may not be able to put in to Bunraha again to let you off."

Mike grasped my arm.

"I'm going with you. Please let me come! I'll be useful on the boat. You can't leave me at home now."

So I agreed to let him come. What else could I do? He had saved us from disaster. He thought of it as a reward for what he had done. And from our experiences since we left home, I could see that a third member in the party might be the difference between life and death for us all.

"But your father—Big Johnny? What will he say?"

"I won't tell him," said Mike simply. "He would never give me leave to go, but if I go and come home safely he'll be boasting about me to the neighbours for the rest of his life."

"But—if we don't get back?"

"We'll get back, all right," said Mike.

He threw the currach's rope into her and pushed her out with the *Wave-Rider's* boat-hook. Then he left only one rope holding the *Wave-Rider*, so that we could get away in a hurry if necessary. He told me to leave my shoes behind, and then we went like a pair of prowling cats up the quay towards the lighthouse.

To get to the lighthouse itself, we had to pass the stone cottages in which the men lived. A light glared from the window of one. We were close enough to see in, to where Pat and Matt were sitting at a table, and the two light-keepers were filling a long canvas bag with clothes. The one who was holding the mouth of the bag open was the one who had captured Joe. The other man's back was to the window.

We slipped past silently, till we came to the base of the tall white lighthouse. From its top the light swept round continuously, green, red and white. A small door led in. Mike had his screwdriver out and had found the screw-heads in a second. Still it seemed an hour before he swung the little hasp over and pushed the door open.

"You must hurry," he said. "When the men have finished packing they may come looking for me. Up you go!"

I stumbled up the metal ladder. Light came down the shaft from above. There were little landings, three of them, at intervals up through the tower. I was panting when I reached the top, where the light was. And there was Joe, lying on the floor, wrists and ankles tied, and with a frightened look turned towards the ladder's top.

I can never forget his face when he saw who had come.

"Michael!" he said.

"Quiet!" I said. "Better not say a word."

I sawed at his bonds with my old penknife. It was chokingly hot in there, though I was surprised that the light was so small. It was no bigger than a candle-flame, but the glass windows all around magnified it so that it could be seen for miles.

When I had cut the cords, it took Joe a full two minutes to learn to walk again. I was afraid to trust him on the ladder until he had rubbed his ankles hard. Even then, I went down first, so that if he fell I should be able to make some shift to save him.

It was a horrid journey downwards. At any moment, I thought, a hand from below might grasp my ankle. But we reached the ground floor in safety, and slipped outside.

Mike was gone. I had a moment of panic. Then I guessed that he had gone back to the boat to be ready for us. I took Joe by the elbow and steered him past the cottages. As we passed, the one light went out. A moment later the door opened. All the men were coming out!

We threw caution to the winds. We tore down to the quay.

"There they go!"

Boots pounded after us.

"Jump!" came Mike's voice from the boat.

It was already cast off, and a foot out from the wall. We jumped, and lay where we fell. Mike gave a mighty shove with the boat-hook. Six feet separated us from the land. Joe leaped up to take the helm, while Mike and I hoisted the mainsail. She filled with the light night wind. A gun flashed from the quay. Matt shouted:

"Follow them! After them!"

Then we heard Pat's voice.

"None of that! Let them go. We'll catch them on the way back."

Then we were carried out of reach of their voices, as we turned out to sea on our way to the lost island at last.

★ XI ★

As soon as we were well away from Fort Island Joe and Mike put their heads together to plan our course. I was quite useless to them, so I thought I had better be the cabin-boy. While they conferred, I got the oil-stove going and cooked a huge meal of potatoes and tinned stew. There was a silent quarter of an hour while we ate, and at the end of it not a scrap remained. In fact, Joe was scraping the potato-pot for forgotten fragments.

Then we hung out lights and had a proper council of war.

Joe was very pleased to have Mike in the party, and he told me kindly, but firmly, that they would manage the boat between them. I was to cook and do odd jobs and perhaps take an occasional watch. Neither of the two sailors had ever made an ocean voyage before. They had both been outside the bay, but only for long enough to have got a great respect for the strength of the wind and the waves. Even now, though it was a fine night, we were clipping along at a surprising rate, making a long wake in the track of the moon.

That first night, I think we were all overawed at the adventure we were undertaking. After our conference, Joe and I lay down to sleep, leaving Mike in charge of the boat. Mike insisted on this, as he was the only one of us who had had a proper night's sleep for days. As I fell asleep, I felt a pang in my throat as I thought of the immensity of the wide seas, and the smallness of our little boat moving across, like a midge on a huge window-pane.

The morning sun made everything look more cheerful. When Mike woke me, I came out of the cabin rubbing my eyes. But after a wash in cold sea-water, I felt livelier, and was able to look around me with delight.

It was a brilliant morning. The sea shone like gold in the sun, and away off astern I could see the outline of Fort Island dim in the haze on the horizon. The boat rode the little waves as a following wind made the sails hum. A seagull was perched on the mast-head, and others sailed in the air behind us, crying their lonesome cry.

I called Joe, and prepared breakfast while he splashed himself with water. We had decided to have no swimming, because of the difficulty of getting in and out of the boat. But now we found that we had no desire to swim. The sea was too big to be inviting.

"I bet Noah and his family didn't go swimming from the Ark," said Joe.

"Very few of the islandmen can swim," said Mike. "They say the sea may be all right for the fishes, but a Christian was meant to stay on dry land. My father is a fine swimmer, though, and he taught me. We get in more wrack between us than any other family."

He told us how after a storm the islanders always go along the clifftops looking out for floating wrack from drowned ships. Whatever a man can bring in is his own.

"Of course the police don't see it that way," he said. "They come out from the mainland sometimes, asking questions, wanting to know where did we get this, that and the other. If we don't want the stuff then, we hand it over to them, but mostly it's useful to ourselves. We're not doing anyone any harm by saving what would be totally lost only for us."

"What sort of things do you get?"

"Baulks of timber, if we're lucky. All our tables and chairs are made of them. Sacks of meal or flour—the sea-water makes a kind of paste on the outside, but inside it's fine and dry. Once we got a whole cargo of sheet rubber. Man, it made great shoes! We thought it would never wear out."

One could see by the easy way he sat at the helm, keeping the boat just close enough to the wind, that Mike was a born man of the sea. He was not afraid of it, as even Joe was. He told us of some marvellous rescues, brought about by the islanders, with a life-line running from the cliff-top to a ship heeled over against the rocks, hounded there by the slavering storm; of the sailors carried up the very face of the cliffs to the warm safety of the islanders' homes. And then in the dawn, when the storm was spent, the islanders would climb down the same cliff-face, to carry up just as tenderly the precious wrack.

"And do the light-keepers come to help you rescue the sailors?" I asked innocently.

"Rescue them? As often as not, they are the cause of the shipwreck!"

We were stricken with horror.

"Do you mean they lead the ships astray?"

"The pair of light-keepers we have now are wreckers," said Mike simply. "Soon after they came, a year ago, we noticed that there were more wrecks than ever before. We never wish for a wreck—we'd let all the wrack go hang to save one sailor's life. Then we noticed that the light-keepers always got to the wreck first. While we were saving the sailors, they were looting the ship. They sold what they got too, which was a thing we never did. A boat used to come out from the town to collect the stuff—a boat belonging to Pat Conway!"

Joe and I looked at each other. It was no wonder that Pat had been shy of the police.

"My father, Big Johnny, wanted to tell the police about it, but the others would not agree. They said the light-keepers would get suspicious if they saw police in Bunraha, where they never come. We had no proof that they really wrecked the ships. Everyone agreed that the best thing would be to catch them at their game red-handed, some night. If we could get even one sailor to swear he saw a light in a place where it had no right to be—then we would have them. But it just happened that all the ships that were wrecked were strangers to these parts. By the time the men had faced death, and been hauled up the cliff on a rope, they could never rightly say what did or did not happen. There's many a Fort Islandman would give a lot to catch those blackguards," said Mike feelingly.

It was just as well we had not known all this when we made our bargain with Pat Conway for his boat. I shuddered to think how narrowly we had escaped their clutches such a short time ago. It all seemed very distant now, with the sun shining and the fair breeze blowing us swiftly along.

Very soon we settled down to our new way of life. We were glad now that we had jerseys and socks to spare, for we were able to give a supply of both to Mike. I was surprised at the cold of the nights until I reflected that only a single plank of teak separated my bunk from the ocean. But this was not a thought to be given house-room for long.

We slept and watched and ate by turns. Our appetites became enormous. When I saw our bags of potatoes and meal dwindling before my eyes, I fixed up a fishing-line and caught some strange-looking fish. They leered at me nastily, even when they were dead, and it took great courage to eat them. Joe brought tears to our eyes with his description of our boat floating on across the world with our three dead bodies stiffened in front of plates of my fish. But Mike said:

"Anything that smells as good as that couldn't but be good to eat."

And he swallowed a large forkful.

We watched him smack his lips with pleasure and prod for more.

"We may as well all die together," said I to Joe. "Hurry, or Mike will have cleared the lot."

Nothing happened, and from then on we ate as many of those fish as we could catch.

When Fort Island dropped behind, we saw no more land. The weather continued to be warm and sunny. Now and then we saw a lone shark basking just under the surface of the water, rolling lazily with one fin up. The sharks were very curious, and always came close to have a look at us. Mike said they sometimes used to get under the currachs and try to upset them, but our boat was too big for that. In any case, the sharks we saw were too lazy to want to exert themselves by teasing us.

One evening, in a calm, we saw a school of porpoises. They ruffled the surface of the water as they swam furiously just under. Sometimes one would give a wild curving leap into the air and land in the water again with a splash. They danced around the boat for a while, and then they shot off at great speed still playing their game. Mike said the Fort Islanders called them "Sea-pigs", but they looked far too athletic to be called pigs, I thought.

That night was Joe's watch on deck. In the dark, towards morning, he came into the cabin for his oilskins. When we got up later on, everything was streaming with water.

We could not see more than a hundred yards, for a low cloud of mist hung over the sea. We were in a dead calm, and it was bitingly cold. For the first time I wondered if we would ever really see that island. Though neither of them said a word, I could see that the other two had reached the same edge of despair.

They had plotted their course well enough, to be sure, and had kept to it. Both of them knew how to do that. But I had never before doubted that that course would lead us to the lost island. I knew the island existed. I clung with all my might to that fact. But the "directions" for getting there! Could anything be more unlikely? North of south and south of north, indeed! Not even a map! And here we were ten days out from Fort Island, and not a sign of a ship nor an island in all that time.

The absence of the ships had not troubled us much, for we had guessed that the lost island was off the main trade routes. And the winds had been light, so that we had not made much headway at times. I comforted myself with these thoughts and tried to look as if everything were turning out just as I had expected. But Joe said, showing that his spirits had really dropped:

"I wish I had brought my rat."

And Mike said:

"I wonder if we should use the engine?"

I would not allow this. Though I was no sailor, I knew that the engine might yet save us from ruin. I said that we must sit there for a week rather than use it too soon.

The curious thing about that calm was the way the mainsail flapped all the time. An oily swell lifted the boat up and down. We sat about in our oilskins waiting for a breeze, while Joe wrote in the little note-book that was our log-book. When I fished, for something to do, I discovered that the shoal of fish that had followed us all the time had departed, and somehow I felt quite lonely for them. As I hauled in my line I said:

"It's too wet even for the fish to-day. They've all gone home."

"No fish?"

Mike jumped up.

"It could mean nothing, but it often means a storm. We'd better lower the jib."

We did, and rolled it up all heavy with rain. We collected our loose gear and stowed it in the cabin, and then we sat inside the open cabin door, Joe and I, looking at Mike as if we expected him to take the storm out of his pocket now that we were ready for it.

Still the boat never moved, and the swell rolled us as if some sea-monster were using the bottom of the boat for a scratching-post. As evening came on the mist turned leaden grey, and when the dark came it had showed no signs of lifting.

After supper Mike and I lay down to sleep, while Joe took the idle helm.

"It could be a false alarm," said Mike. "Call us if things get lively."

I woke hours later to feel the *Wave-Rider* tearing along. The water chuckled and cheered about her, and she rose and fell on the waves true to her name. Mike had lit the lantern and was getting into his clothes.

"She shouldn't be doing as well as this," he said. "I have an idea we'll all be wanted soon."

I pulled on my clothes and followed him outside. It was still night. The sky was full of ragged clouds, bitten in shreds by a high roaring wind. The mist was gone, and the dim glow of moonlight shone on a tossing, foaming wilderness of water. Spray from the wave-tops blew into the boat on a raw wind. Sometimes her bows struck the middle of a wave with a sickening little whack. Then she seemed to pause and shudder before going on again.

"A dirty enough night," said Mike. "I hope it gets no worse than this."

He took over the helm from Joe, who was relieved to

part with it. Then Joe and I reefed the mainsail, but our pace scarcely diminished at all.

"That's all the better," said Mike. "It would be a shame to waste the wind. And if we don't keep some way on the boat, we can't handle her at all."

How glad I was now that Mike had come with us! He made use of every squall to teach us how to manœuvre the boat. He explained why a beam sea was liable to fill the boat or capsize her, and that a zig-zag course kept the wind always forward or aft of our beam. He showed us how to luff up to the rollers, and he praised the lively way the boat's head came past the wind when he put down the helm. But all the time, deep down in me, I was promising myself that when this voyage would be over, I would be an armchair sailor for evermore. It was exciting, to be sure, but it was the same kind of dangerous excitement I had felt when the horse I was riding bolted. And one does not ride a bolting horse for choice.

Presently the dawn came up on an angry sea. The wind had strengthened, and Mike commented that we looked like having a busy day. His eyes glowed at the prospect.

"I love a good storm," he said mischievously, in answer to my look. "They say all the Conneeleys are really seals in disguise. That would be why we're such good swimmers too."

I got together a sort of meal, though I could not light the stove. We had to feed Mike as he stood at the helm, for he would not trust either of us to take it over from him. Joe had not spoken for some time; he had been looking away on our starboard side. Now he turned and said quietly:

"I think I see land!"

Mike jerked the helm, so that the boat heeled over dangerously. When he had righted her again he looked very shamefaced.

"It seems to me you'd be better with a seal at the helm," he said.

We gazed in the direction of Joe's pointing finger, which shook with excitement.

"I've been watching it for ten minutes," he said, trying to speak calmly. "It's quite hard to make out if it is land at all, on account of the waves."

"It's the lost island," I said softly. "I know it is!"

"It's not any place I ever saw before," said Mike cautiously. "We could be off our course, but I don't think we are. I sailed to Cornwall and Brittany once, with my father, and it doesn't look like any place I saw then."

We watched it for twenty minutes, while we tacked laboriously towards it. Now we could see that it was an island, all right. But whether it was our island we had no way of knowing. It was high at one end, and it had a long flat piece at the other. The day had brightened a little, and the island was a dark-blue hump on the darker blue angry water. As we came nearer we could see a threatening line of white from end to end of it.

"It looks like a bad place to land on, sure enough," said Joe. "I don't see a single break in the line of surf. It looks as if there is no harbour."

"Perhaps there is one on the other side," said Mike. "Now we'll need that engine to keep us off the lee shore. Without it we would be blown on to the island like a stone from a catapult."

I filled our petrol tank and started the engine, to try it out. We had a moment of agony while it spluttered a little. Then it settled down to a steady hum. I switched it off. I wanted to shout and wave my arms with excitement. We must be—we were coming to the lost island at last.

During the next six hours I had plenty of time to calm down. Though we were moving towards the island in short tacks, it seemed to get no nearer. I even thought at one time that it was moving away and away from us, leading us like a will-o'-the-wisp to destruction.

But the experienced sailors, Joe and Mike, said that we were getting nearer, and I tried to smother my impatience. We were thankful that the wind had not got any stronger, for even as it was the boat needed very careful handling. The tacking made our progress very slow.

In the afternoon I went and lay down in the cabin. I was certain I would not be able to sleep, and I did not want to leave my post watching the island. But Joe and Mike insisted that one of us would have to rest, so as to be ready for hard work later on. As I was the least knowledgeable sailor, I could best be spared. Within a few minutes I slept like a stone.

I woke to find Joe shaking me. I sprang up, and out of the cabin. I paused to stare. We were quite close to the island now, perhaps a quarter of a mile away, and we were approaching it rapidly. The high end of it was composed of brownish-grey rock, with long fingers of reefs tossed off from it into the sea. The waves raced and broke over the reefs and made little whirlpools farther out where there were submerged rocks. The flatter end of the island was bordered with low sheer cliffs. The spray from the waves dashed over the top of them and was carried away across the island in a cloud, on the wind. At the base of the cliffs was the white line we had seen from the distance. Near at hand it took on terrifying proportions.

"Stand by to start the engine," said Mike. "We're on the weather side, and I've just felt a current dragging us to the reefs."

"You're the captain, Mike," said I. "We'll jump to your orders!"

I started up the engine. Joe lowered the mainsail. Though Mike kept the helm hard down, the current was so strong that I thought we were going to be dashed to pieces against the cliffs. But just in time we came round in a curve and headed out to sea again.

Mike wiped the sweat off his forehead. I looked back at the island, and it seemed that the waves were shouting:

"We'll get you next time! Haaa! We'll get you next time!"

Now we had to get the boat round fast enough, so as not to take the waves broadside on. Mike decided to avoid the rocky end of the island, on account of the current and the reefs.

"You never know with reefs," he said. "When you think you have passed them all, there's often another one just under the water waiting to strand you."

When we got out half a mile, we hoisted the mainsail again and switched off the engine. We sailed around the flat end of the island to the lee side. We moved closer in, and wondered at the amount of shelter the island afforded. For a hundred yards out from the land, the water was almost calm, except for a wrinkle and scurry on its flat surface. We sailed quite close in and lowered our sail again. Then we started up the engine and began to look for a landing place.

There were cliffs on this side as on the other, sheer and unbroken. We passed along slowly, straining our eyes for any sign of a harbour. There was none. We went along the whole way, to where the reefs started again, and to where the tearing winds and thundering waves could be heard pounding the rocks at the island's head.

But there was no place where we could land.

It was a cruel disappointment. Where were all my theories now? How grandly I had told Joe that there was a little difficulty about landing on the island! How sure I had been that we would be able to surmount that difficulty!

We brought the boat back to the middle of the island, and switched off the engine without a word. Joe dropped the anchor. The water was a dull opaque blue, so that we could not see the sea-bottom, but the anchor held.

It was perhaps six o'clock by now. Sailing round the island had taken time. It seemed that we might have to spend the night here. Mike stood up and began to peel off his jacket.

"I'm going to swim ashore," he said.

"Wait!" said Joe. "There's some sort of animal on the cliff-top. I saw it just now. Look!"

There was a movement of something white there. We all craned forward to look, but it was gone again.

"Was it a flag?" said Mike.

"No," said Joe. "I'm sure it was an animal. I saw it run towards the high end."

"What animal could it be? Surely there aren't bears as far South as this," I said.

"Bears!" said Mike. "Perhaps I won't swim ashore after all."

We looked uncertainly at each other. Then Joe said in a dead voice:

"Perhaps it's not the lost island at all!"

Suddenly I saw the white thing again, nearer this time. I leaped on to the cabin roof.

"It's a man! It's a man in queer white clothes!"

The others jumped up beside me.

"He sees us! Look! He's waving his arms!"

He was waving his arms, and dancing up and down. He was shouting now. His voice came, clear as a bird-call on the wind:

"Michael! Is that you, Michael?"

It was the other two who waved and danced and thouted, though their voices were carried away at once on she wind, and he could not have heard them. I was sitting down on the cabin roof, dizzy and speechless and unable to think of anything.

The others dragged me to my feet, caught my hands and held me up for my father to see.

"Wave, Michael!" they shouted in my ear.

And at last I managed to do so. I was amazed to find tears on my face.

The voice came again, clear and high:

"Land over there!"

And he pointed to the end of the island, where we had seen that the cliffs rose as sheer as they did where we were anchored.

We looked at each other in astonishment. How could he suggest such a thing? I wondered for a moment if his mind had become affected by his long stay alone on the island. But he was waving again and calling something, and running along the cliff-top towards the end of the island.

"He's going to lead us to a place where we can land," said Mike, beginning to haul in the anchor.

"But shouldn't we wait till the storm dies down?" I said doubtfully. "He was pointing towards the weather side of the island. It will be no use if we all get cast away and the boat gets broken up."

"The storm might last for weeks," said Mike. "And anyway, I wouldn't call this little blow a storm. It might get forty times worse, and then we'd be in trouble, for sure."

"If it gets worse", said Joe, "this place where we're so nicely sheltered won't be much use to us. This is our chance to land."

So once more we got our engine going. We followed the white figure along the cliff to the point. He directed us to keep close in there, and though it seemed like madness, we did. And then we saw the most astonishing thing of all.

At the tip of the island, just where a few yards more

would have sent us to destruction by the storm, a narrow corridor of water opened up between the cliffs. It was impossible to see it from any distance out, because an outcropping of rock almost covered the entrance, leaving just enough room for our boat to slip through.

Inside the water was as still as glass and it was curiously quiet. On either side, cliff walls rose directly above us, and below we could see their wavering sides going down and down through the clear green sea.

Overawed, we said not a word as we traversed the passageway. It curved a little in front, so that we could not see where it ended. We rounded the curve, and our amazement was complete.

We were in a little circular harbour. There were cliffs on both sides, but they sloped away before us rapidly to a shingly beach. We switched off the engine and let the boat glide in. Only vaguely now we heard the sound of the sea, so that I guessed the corridor had led in towards the middle of the island. To one side of the beach, some rocks formed a natural pier, and Mike, with the islander's genius, made straight for these. We gripped the rock with our hands and brought the boat to a standstill.

And now the moment I had dreamed of was here at last. Down along the rocks came the man in the queer white clothes. I climbed ashore and went forward slowly to meet my father.

★ XII ★

It was a few minutes before I remembered that Mike and Joe were standing in the boat watching us. They were grinning from ear to ear. We made fast the boat and they leaped ashore, and I introduced them to my father.

After those first minutes, it was as if he had never been away at all. He looked very different, to be sure, with his beard and darkly sunburned face. And he was dressed in a sort of jacket and trousers made of white fur. He laughed when he saw us staring at him.

"You must have thought I was a polar bear when you saw me first," he said. "I'll tell you all about that later on."

Before we went a step, I had to tell him that my mother was well, and that the farm was prospering. I told him about Billy, and how he had retrieved our fortunes when it had looked as if all was lost.

Suddenly we all felt very tired. The ground under my feet seemed to rock with the motion of the boat.

"You must come to my house at once," said my father. "If you have any food on board, it will probably be better than what I can offer you."

So we loaded ourselves with stores, and then made our way up the beach. At the top there was a level patch of sand, and the opening of a cave.

"My house!" said my father grandly. "Come inside."

The cave was almost round. It was perhaps ten feet in diameter, and had a good dry high roof. Against one wall there was a bed made of a heap of carrageen, a kind of spongy white dried seaweed. It was covered with more of the white fur, and a roll of blankets lay at one end. There was a roughly-made table and a bench, and some shelves with cups and plates, and a few books.

"This is a wonderful place! There's many a house isn't as cosy as this," said Mike.

"We took a lot of things off our boat," said my father. "It's a long story. We must have supper first."

He smacked his lips over the tinned stew. It was a pleasant change from seal-meat, he said.

After we had finished we brought our beds from the boat and arranged them in the cave, for we had decided to sleep on dry land. We brought our lantern too, and placed it on a convenient ledge.

"We'll just have time to look at my garden before darkness falls," said my father.

He led us out of the cave and between some standing rocks, and we came out on the rim of a little valley. A large patch of it had been sown with potatoes, which were in a far more advanced state of growth than ours had been when I had left home.

"Potatoes do well by the sea," he said. "The small plants are peas. They're not very well on yet. Potatoes and peas—that has been my diet, with seal-meat and shellfish and carrageen and an odd rockfish."

"But how did you manage to plant these?" I asked, still amazed at the flourishing crops.

"We had potatoes on board, and dried peas. We were sorely tempted to eat them all that first winter, but we forced ourselves to keep them for seed instead. They saved our lives later, I'm certain."

We said no more till we were back in the cave again. With the lantern lit and a white skin drawn across the doorway to keep out the cold night air, it was a pleasant

place, and we settled down to listen to the whole story of my father's adventures.

They had had a fair wind all the way. Their boat was bigger than ours, and was able to make better time, and they sighted the island on the morning of the seventh day. They sailed all round it, but like us, they failed to find the only place where they could have landed. They anchored off the reefs for the night, intending to swim ashore and explore the island in the morning. But when they woke in the morning, the island was lost in fog. They were unable to move. All day they waited for the fog to lift, and the next day, and the next. Then Tomeen began to get nervous. He said Manannan had seen them and had made the island invisible. He said they must get away from the place at once, for it was full of evil. My father argued with him for hours, but he would not listen. He stayed awake all the time, straining his eyes and ears towards where the island had been, refusing to eat or rest. My father watched him all the time, for fear he would do something foolish. This went on until they had been anchored by the island for five days. Then my father, being quite exhausted, fell asleep where he sat.

"Tomeen was quite unbalanced by now," he said. "He hauled in the anchor very quietly and hoisted the sails. He must have turned the boat straight into the current, for I woke up from my doze when we crashed into the reef. And there we hung.

"Tomeen was aghast at what he had done. By the way the boat was settling on the reef I knew that she was holed. I climbed out into the water, but I could see nothing. It was half a day more, in the evening, before the fog lifted.

"It rolled away like a stage curtain, and there was the island, glittering in the blue sea, and the sun going down in a golden blaze behind it. But it was no use to us now.

The tide had gone down, and there we were, high and dry on the rocks.

"It was well for us that we had struck at high tide; then the cabin floor had been awash with sea water, but when the tide went down it was dry again. Tomeen lay on his bed in there now, in a fever, raving about Mannanan, who was coming to get him. I climbed out on to the rocks again, and examined the hole.

"It was towards the bows, on the port side, and it was pretty bad. I knew hardly anything about ship-building, but I was something of a carpenter, and I could see that some new planks would have to be put in before she would be fit to sail home. And we could not stay on the rocks while this was being done. I gave Tomeen some brandy, and he fell into a kind of doze. I thought it quite possible that if he woke he would try to wreck the boat further, but I had to risk that. I walked up the rocks to explore the island, before the tide would come up again.

"I do not know what I expected to find. Mannanan seated on a mother-o'-pearl throne, perhaps, surrounded by mermaids. I know I was very apprehensive until I had covered as much of the island as possible. Then I climbed to its highest point and looked about me. It was quite deserted.

"It was from this point that I saw the anchorage. I made my way down there and went over it all. I saw that I could make the cave habitable, and a good fresh-water stream ran through the valley and down over the rocks to the sea.

"I got back to the boat just as the tide reached it again. Tomeen was still asleep, but he soon woke up and I could see that he was worse. The cabin was damp and the water was coming through again, but I could not move him. I sat waiting for the tide to fall again, and hoping that we would not be lifted off the rocks by a high sea.

"The delay every time the tide came up made all the next part of the work very slow. First I had to carry blankets ashore and make a bed for Tomeen in the cave. Then I brought food and cups and cutlery and other things I thought would be useful. I tried to fix the cave to look like home, because I could see we were going to have to live there for a long time. That it would be four years I had no idea.

"All the time I prayed that there would not be a storm before I could save the boat.

"At last I got Tomeen ashore somehow. It was the worst journey I have ever undertaken. I dragged over the rocks with him, and climbed on to the shore, and then there was the long rocky way to the cave. He fought me when he saw that I was taking him to the island, but he was very feeble, and I was more than a match for him. He was still raving about Manannan.

"We were both exhausted when we reached the cave. I gave him more brandy and tried to make him comfortable, and soon he fell asleep. I was afraid to waste time, and I went straight back to the boat for more of our things. I took the toolbox that time, and all the portable gear of the boat. I brought load after load to the shore, and at last the boat was stripped bare. I spent the rest of the day transferring the stuff to the cave. When I had brought the last load I gave Tomeen a drink and covered him up warmly. And then I lay down on my own bed and slept like one dead.

"The next few days were divided between nursing Tomeen and trying to save the boat. I knew very little about ship-building, as I have said, and I could only try to imagine what one could do to patch up a leaking boat.

"I took my own oilskin coat and cut a patch out of it to fit the hole. I pressed the splintered wood together as much as I could and nailed the oilskin on top. Now my trouble was to make the edges waterproof. We had some oil, but it was not heavy enough, and when I put it on the edges of the oilskin it ran straight off again. We had butter, but not enough to go all round the patch.

"Finally I picked some carrageen up off the shore, where it had dried of itself. I boiled it in a little sea water, and when it was cold it was a soft jelly, which I mixed with the butter to make it go farther. I baled all the water out of the boat at low tide, and plastered the mixture around the edges of the patch. Then I had to wait for the tide to come up again, to see if my plan would work.

"While I was waiting I got an oar ready, for I would have to use it to help me off the rocks. The boat was too wide for one person to be able to use both oars together. The breeze was light, for which I was thankful, for I had a superhuman task before me.

"I lashed the helm hard over, so that it would keep the course of the boat straight. I meant to push the boat off the rocks stern first, with the boat-hook. Then I climbed out on to the rocks, and tried to remove as many stones as would leave a sort of channel, in which the boat was to move off. I was fairly successful in doing this, but the rising tide cut my work short.

"How I actually achieved my carefully laid plan now seems to me to have been a miracle. With the stones removed, I soon felt her stern lifting. I held my patience until the tide was on the turn, for I had noticed that the current was not so strong then. Now I went forward with the boat-hook and shoved, and perhaps because she was lighter with all her gear removed, she soon lifted free.

"Have you ever tried to row a heavy sailing-boat stern first against the current? I don't know how I did it. All I can say is that after half an hour of agonizing labour, we were ten feet off the reef, floating between the current and the island. Now I shifted my oar to the other side and brought the boat round in a curve. Then I loosened my knot and eased the helm to amidships.

"Now I was able to hoist the mainsail, and I nearly wept with joy when I felt the boat begin to move gently forward. It was well for me that it was a following wind, for tacking would have been out of the question.

"I dared not leave my post to see how my patch was faring. I reflected that I would know soon enough if the boat began to fill, and I was prepared to swim for it then. But it seemed to be holding together, I knew not how, and we were moving slowly nearer to the mouth of the anchorage.

"You saw as you came in how close your boat goes to the cliffs at that place. As we came near I decided to change my plan. I had meant to row the boat through the long corridor, but my experience of that had made me wonder if it would be wise to try it. By the reef, there had been plenty of room to manœuvre the boat, but in the corridor one false jerk might smash my new patch against the cliffs.

"I fixed a long line in the bows and tied the end of it around my waist. Just as I turned into the corridor's mouth I lowered the sail and left it sprawling. Then I leaped for the cliff on the starboard side, where it slopes a little.

"I clung there, feeling sick and terrified, and afraid to look down. The boat had moved into the corridor and the line was gently inrolling. I held on with all my might. My handgrips and footholds were scarcely perceptible and I waited momentarily for the jerk that would send me into the water. When the line was all out there was a long drag, and I closed my eyes.

"I was afraid to move for a few seconds, but at last I pulled gently on my rope. The boat moved backwards a little. Now I had to start climbing the face of the cliff, very slowly and carefully. I pulled at the line now and then, but I had to keep the bows of the boat pointing in along the corridor. I had deliberately left the helm swinging free.

"At last I reached the cliff-top, and rested on the short prickly grass for a few minutes. Then I began to walk along the top, towing the boat, like a barge-horse.

"That was how I got the boat to safety. I beached her just below the cave, on the opposite end of the strand from where your boat is now. I was not able to get her above high water mark alone, but I felt that she was reasonably safe in such a sheltered place. I moored her to the rocks and resolved to spend my time now in bringing Tomeen back to health.

"He lay there for three weeks. I did not know what to do for him. The food we had was wrong for a sick man, and at last the only thing he could eat was carrageen boiled in water. We had brought some tinned milk, but not much. From the safety of home it had seemed like a luxury.

"At last he began to get better; but he was very weak and he could only lie there by the hour looking out of the door of the cave. I told him all I had done, and that the boat was safe. I carried him out into the sun so that he could see her lying there on the beach. I told him that we would be able to mend her ourselves, as soon as he was well.

"And now I discovered a terrible thing. The shock of being cast away on the island, as well as his illness, had affected Tomeen's mind. It was some time before I was sure of this. Now that he was getting well, I tried to leave him for a while, to explore the island and try to improve our position. He would not let me go. I tried to reason with him, but it was no use. He babbled about Manannan, and clutched me. At last I agreed to stay with him all the time, until he would be well enough to come with me.

"I spent some of the time in examining the damage to the boat. My patch held firm, but of course we could not set out for home held together with butter and carrageen and oilskin. The only wood we had was in the shelves and cupboards that had been in the cabin, and which I had transferred to the cave.

"They are there on the walls now. Just look at them! They were quite useless for mending a boat—thin, soft wood that you could punch a hole in with your hands. There were no trees growing on the island. Nothing grew there except grass, and the sea-pinks with their stiff dry leaves, through which the wind whispered. Our only hope was wrack.

"Mike, here, will understand that. But wrack in summer is very scarce, and anyway Tomeen would not let me go to look for it.

"So the weeks dragged on. Our food ran low. I was able to make Tomeen understand that we must keep the potatoes and peas for seed, and we laid them away and tried to forget we had them. Our oil was nearly gone too, and I did not like the prospect of spending a long cold winter on the island with neither fire nor light.

"At last Tomeen was able to walk about, and one day we set out together to explore the island.

"It was that day that we reached the stretch of rocks at the far end of the island, and found the treasure of Manannan."

We all jumped up, and Mike and I shouted:

"Treasure!"

"So there is treasure," said Joe quietly.

"There was treasure, sure enough," my father went on. "I laughed when I saw it, it was so unexpected.

"All over the rocks were sprawling—white seals! There were hundreds of them. They did not see us, for we kept behind a big rock at the top of the sloping shore. We were able to peep out at them to our heart's content.

"There seemed to be different kinds of seals, and I tried to remember all I had ever heard about them. There were big bulls, fat fellows with long fierce moustaches, each with about a dozen wives. The bulls kept up a furious barking noise, especially when another bull came near. We saw two engage in a bloody battle, from which the trespasser departed bellowing, his white coat covered with blood. On the edge of the sea were the younger male seals, called bachelors, who played in and out of the water, and laughed, as I thought, at private jokes among themselves. The pups were down by the sea too, bleating to each other and flopping about. They were fairly well grown, for it was August now, and they had probably been born in June. Their mothers went up and down before them, looking, from the back, like fussy old ladies with long skirts.

"I have called the noise they made barking, and bleating, and roaring. It was all of these things. I realized now that I had heard it from the cave sometimes, but I had thought it was the sea pounding on the rocks.

"As soon as I saw the seals, I knew that, with luck, they would save our lives. Tomeen was tired now, and we had to go home, but we resolved to come here again in the morning.

"The next day we set out for the seal-ground well prepared. We had a short thick stick, a sharp knife and my tin whistle which I had brought to amuse myself on the voyage.

"We placed ourselves this time out of sight behind a rock at the end of the only patch of sand on that part of the shore. I got out my whistle and began to play tunes on it—'The Rocks of Bawn', and 'Haste to the Wedding', and 'The Galbally Farmer'.

"Immediately I began to play a bachelor seal looked up. He cocked his head to listen. Then he got down solemnly off his rock and began to waddle slowly towards us. A moment later another followed suit, and another. Presently there was a procession of seals along the sand. I tootled on. The first one came round the rock. Tomeen whacked him on the nose with his stick and knocked him senseless. We finished him off with the knife, and dragged him away just before the next one arrived.

"At the end of a busy half-hour, my mouth was dry from blowing into the whistle, but a dozen seals lay there at our feet. I felt quite sorry for them, because their big, round, curious eyes and drooping moustaches reminded me so much of Corny Murphy, the grocer at home. The expression on their faces as they peeped around the rock was just like Corny's when he peeps out of his kitchen door while his wife serves you at the shop counter.

"We dragged them one by one to a place where an overhanging rock would shelter them a little, and went home exhausted.

"Next morning we went early to where we had left the seals. We brought the boat's spare water-tank with us, and a good knife each. Then we set about skinning the seals. I had never done this before, but Tomeen had, and under his instruction I found it quite easy. Just under the skin there was a layer of fat, and we put this into the water-tank. Later the oil ran out of it, and we used it for light and cooking. It smelt very badly, but we were so glad to have it that we cared nothing for that.

"We washed out the skins in sea-water, so that the salt would preserve them. We kept some of the flippers, for Tomeen said they were a great delicacy. Then we cut steaks, which we salted later in sea-water. Tomeen was splendid at all this work. Only in one way did he show that his mind was a little unbalanced. He was certain that if he

went about alone, Manannan would catch him and make an end of him. I soon gave up arguing with him on this point.

"Before October we had a couple of hundred sealskins put away, and enough seal-meat salted to do us for the winter. The meat was ugly stuff, with a fishy taste, but we had no choice. I got quite used to it in the end.

"The curious thing was that the seals never seemed to notice that any of them who came to investigate our music never came back.

"At last the weather became cold and dark, and we began to haul our skins back to the cave. We had partly dried them by spreading them on the rocks in the sun. We had built a shelter of stone for them, for the seagulls took a great interest in them. We built a bigger one nearer home, and stowed them all inside.

"Now we had plenty of work for the winter. On every good day, we put the skins out to dry. Then they were all crackly and stiff. Next we took them one by one and rubbed them between our hands to soften them. We found sandy stones, too, with which the rub down any roughness on the skin. It took the whole winter to get through them all.

"The fur was beautifully soft and white, as you can see, except for long hairs of a darker colour which grew all through it. The roots of these long hairs, we found, came right through the skin. When we had scraped the skins clean we singed the roots, and then we were able to brush the long hairs out. It was very slow work, but when it was done the skins were like white velvet.

"All through the winter, those seals never left the island. We used to hear their barking above the howling of the wind. I think they must be the only ones in the world—at least, I have never heard of any other seals who remained white when they were full grown.

"We did not spend the whole winter attending to the

sealskins. After each storm we used to search the coast on the weather side hoping to find some wood with which to mend our boat. Once we found a bag of wheat, which was more to us than gold. We found a little chest of tea, too, and a box with half a dozen soaked teddy-bears inside. Tomeen kept them, for company, he said.

"But we found no wood. Once a baulk of it sailed by so close I thought I could have touched it, but the current swept it away. It was no use trying to follow it.

'In the autumn, a kind of long, thick seaweed like a stick, had been washed in on the shore. I don't know the proper name for it, but in Irish it is called 'Slat Mara', which means simply 'Sea Stick'. We collected a good many of these and dried them, and used them for making fires. They burned slowly, sometimes only smouldering, and we would have given a lot for a rick of good black Connemara turf. We kept every splinter of wood from the tea-chest, and any boxes we could spare, to be used as kindling.

"Tomeen always looked after the fire, and he could nearly make the stones burn, as I told him. He was very proud of this, and it was this same faculty that delayed our task of mending the boat for a long time.

"One morning, at the end of the winter, we found some wood on the western side of the island, under the cliffs. There had been no storm, and there was no reason why it should be there. But there it was, two separate planks, bobbing up and down quietly, a yard apart. I spent the whole morning fishing for them, lying on my chest on the cliff-top trailing a loop on the end of a rope. After a hundred disappointments, I hauled one and then the other up the face of the cliff.

"They were long planks, not too thick, and just the thing for our purpose. We took one each and hauled them home, singing all the way. We laid them out on stones to dry in the breeze.

"It occurred to me that there might be other things floating in the neighbourhood of the island. Tomeen had been better lately, and he agreed that I should go to prospect while he prepared a meal. I took my rope and went off, and I spent the best part of two hours scanning the sea from the cliff-top, without success.

"When I felt hungry, I turned to go home. A quarter of a mile away I heard it, unmistakably. It was the sound of the axe on wood. I flew home like a hawk plunging on his prey. But I was too late. Tomeen had just finished making kindling of the last of the second plank.

"He pointed to it proudly, and said that now we would have enough kindling for next winter. He looked so pleased that I could not scold him. I simply remarked that I had thought of mending the boat with that timber!

"No more timber came in. We spent the summer in collecting more sealskins and in laying by meat for the next winter. We planted the potatoes and peas too, having manured the ground with seaweed, as they do all around the coast at home. We got splendid crops, and it was wonderful to taste new potatoes again.

"It was in the autumn that I found the pearls. Near the seal-ground, another stream flowed into the sea, and the seals often ate a kind of grey-shelled mollusc that lived there. I found the shells strewn about, and thought that the fish should make good food for us too. It was only when we began to collect them that I found that many of them contained a very perfect, pear-shaped pearl.

"I have over a thousand of them put away, to bring home.

"Another winter and summer passed, and still no timber came in. It was as if, having wasted our opportunity, we were not to have another. We had got so used to living on the island now that we had even achieved a certain degree of comfort.Our clothes began to wear out, and we made others of the sealskins. We put our own away carefully, so that we would have proper clothes in which to go home. The winters were not harsh here, though the winds were so strong that we dared not venture out of our sheltered valley for weeks at a time.

"At the end of the third summer, in September it was, we found some wood on the shore again. There was much more of it this time. I gave some of it to Tomeen for kindling, and put away some for myself, telling him not to touch it.

"And now at last I was able to set about mending the boat. Tomeen got very excited when he saw me at work, wanting me to hurry so that we could leave all the sooner. I explained to him that it would be madness to attempt the trip home in winter, with a patched-up boat. He did not seem able to understand this. At last I hid the remainder of the wood and pretended that I had not enough to finish the job.

"But Tomeen had been a carpenter at home. He had lost his skill completely since his illness, but now he began to fumble at the boat, trying out ways of finishing off the work with makeshift material. At last I saw that the only thing to do was to finish the patch, and moor the boat out from the shore where he would not be able to reach it, for he was a very poor swimmer. I did this, and explained my reasons to him, and told him that in the first fine weather of spring, we would go home. I moored the boat and swam ashore, and tried to keep my patience till we would be off.

"How Tomeen reached that boat, and got it through the corridor to the sea, I will never discover. I started awake towards the dawn one morning and found he had gone from the cave. I rushed outside to find that the boat had vanished. I ran along the cliff-top, and reached the mouth of the corridor to find that he had already hoisted the sails, and was putting out to sea. I called to him to come back, but he sat like a statue at the helm. I knew he must have heard me, for a strong wind was blowing his way. I made a trumpet of my hands and shouted to him to tell Michael to come for me, and then I could do no more. I watched him till he was part of the sea.

"Back at the cave, I found that he had managed to get some potatoes and a water-barrel to the boat, when my back was turned. I was relieved at this, for I had feared for him on the open sea without food or water. He had brought his teddy-bears, and I soon discovered that he had taken the lantern too, and the oil-stove, but he had left me some oil. I now had to make a light by hanging a wick on the edge of a saucerful of oil, and I had to try to make a new way of cooking on something like the same lines. Later I found that he had taken my horn-handled knife too, which he had always admired.

"Poor Tomeen! I never thought of blaming him. I knew his mind was gone, and I only hoped he would reach home safely, where I felt sure he would come back to his usual health again. But the seas were heavy and the winds were high, and I thought it more than likely that he would never reach home at all.

"I believe that there are few men who could have survived that sail home in storm and cold, single-handed, and with scanty food. Tomeen was a good-hearted fellow. His last thought was for me, as your friend Mikus Kavanagh showed. It's no use now wishing that he had waited for the fine weather in the spring."

★ XIII ★

There was a long silence when my father had finished his story. Then Joe said:

"So the teddy-bears were drowned after all."

Mike said:

"If you could have made smoke, or put up a flag, surely some passing boat would have seen you."

"We did neither," said my father. "Perhaps we could have taken the mast out of the boat and hung a sealskin on it. Anyway we never saw a ship near us. They seem to avoid this neighbourhood."

"It's a bad place for fogs, they say," said Michael.

"One thing I don't understand," I said. "Why did my mother not report what had happened and get a search party after you?"

"That was my own doing," said my father ruefully. "Before I went I made her swear to tell no one where I had gone. I was certain that the voyage would be a success, you see. And I didn't want to be laughed at. Neither did I want a search party to arrive in the middle of my treasure-hunting. Oh, I've had plenty of time to regret all that foolishness."

"But you found the treasure, all right," said Joe.

We were all very tired by now, and we wasted no time in rolling into our beds, to sleep soundly till morning.

It was strange in the morning to find that it was all real, that we were actually asleep in a cave on a desert island, and that the man coming in at the door dressed in sealskins was my own father. He had been about long before us, and had been down to examine the boat. The storm had blown away to the westward, so that we were able to make plans for our departure.

"We'll have to pack sealskins into every nook and cranny," said my father. "I think we'll fit a good many. There's space under the floor-boards; and we can tie a bale of them on to the cabin top."

There was a misty pink now where the sun had risen, and we could hardly hear the soft slow wash of the little waves on the beach of the anchorage.

"It's a fine thing to see a real boat moored there," said my father.

Now we set to work to make the boat ready for our return journey. Joe and my father overhauled all the rigging and sails, while Mike and I carried bale after bale of sealskins on board. We stuffed them in singly, everywhere they would fit. We ended with a tall bale of them on the cabin roof, as my father had suggested, and another on the deck. We fixed the one on the roof with two ropes, which we would cut through if we met with heavy seas and the bale became a danger.

When we had packed in the skins we brought fresh water on board. We had enough food to take us home, and we would be able to fish as we had done on the way out. I asked my father if we would bring some seal-meat, but the look of disgust on his face was answer enough. He said:

"When I get home, every time I look at Corny Murphy I will know what he would taste like if I cut a steak off him!"

It was evening before we had finished, and we thought it better to spend a last night on the island. Though we said nothing, all three of us noticed that my father got up many times during the night to make sure that the boat was safe.

In the morning we brought our bedding down to the boat and stowed it away.

"You'd better not go home dressed like Robinson Crusoe," I said to my father. "Have you still got the clothes you kept for going home?"

He had, but they were very worn. We found a jersey almost big enough to fit him. He wriggled his arms up and down and said:

"I hope it will stretch soon. I never before knew how comfortable the sealskin clothes were. It would be rather nice to be able to wear them always."

I laughed to think of the excitement they would cause among our quiet neighbours.

We left the sealskin suit in the cave. We tore a page from our log-book, and my father wrote a letter to anyone who might be cast away on the island. He told where the salted meat was, and that there were potatoes and peas in the garden. He advised the reader to keep some for seed, as he had done. He oiled his knife against rust, and left it on top of the letter, in the middle of the cave's floor.

"I'll leave my shelves too, and my cups and plates, and a can of oil," he said. "I hope no one will ever need to use them."

Now we were ready to go. My father reached into a recess at the back of the cave, and took out a stout little canvas bag.

"The pearls," he said.

He plunged his hand in, and lifted up some to show us. They were very perfect in shape, but rather dull. He said that by the time they would appear in the jewellers' shops, they would look very different.

"I would almost like to go and say good-bye to the seals," said my father. "They were my best friends, though

I treated them so badly. There was one female there, that I christened Mary Ann. She was very tame, and I had thought of bringing her here later on and milking her, if she would let me. Now it looks as if I'll never taste seal's milk!"

"One can't have everything," said Mike sardonically.

My father looked around his cave for the last time, as if he wanted to fix it in his memory, and then we started down to the boat.

We used the engine to go through the corridor. Now that we were on our way home, we planned to use it if we got becalmed too, for now we would not have to be so very sparing of the petrol. We nosed our way out of the corridor, and hoisted our mainsail and jib. We turned out to sea, and the wind sang a song of home in the sails. The sea was deep blue, with small waves. A golden line of sun streaked away behind us. We looked back at the island, which was already growing smaller, ringed with gold. A line of mist stole in between as we watched, and then we saw the island "Floating between the sea and the sky", as old Bartley had said.

A strange thing happened then. Though the sun still shone all around us, the line of mist lifted itself up and stretched, until it quite covered the island from our view. We could not even see a thickness in the mist where it had been. We watched for a long time, but it did not appear again. That was the last we saw of the lost island.

The voyage home was very different from the outward one. The weather was sunny and clear, with a strong following wind. The feeling of uneasiness and black danger was gone. My father's presence gave us confidence, so that we sailed the *Wave-Rider* as if it were a toy. The extra hand made the work far less, and there was always time for a concert and a song. We learned to hop over and around our cargo so that it did not trouble us in the least. Our shoal of fish came back, and in the still evenings the porpoises leaped and played all around us. Sometimes we saw the ominous fin of a shark, cutting the surface of the water and then disappearing silently, mysteriously. If it could be like this always, I thought, I might even take to the sea again some time.

On the fifth day we saw two steamers. My father had altered our course so that we would come into the regular trade route. We must land at Bunraha to let Mike off before going on home.

I remembered something suddenly.

"Pat Conway said he would get us on the way home," I said.

"About time you mentioned it," said my father. "It won't do to sail into a trap."

Mike explained that the light-keepers had been suspected of wrecking.

"They'll probably change the light if we arrive at night," he said. "They have a powerful telescope that they take up to the top of the tower. They can see us coming miles away through that."

"And what if we arrive in daylight?"

"They'll have some other trick then, you may be sure," said Mike. "They are never short of ideas."

"I was badly taken in by one of their ideas myself," said Joe.

"Then we'll make sure to arrive at night," said my father. "It's a great thing to know what your enemy is planning to do."

"But if we come in in daylight we'll be able to see what they are doing," I objected. "Wouldn't that be better?"

"And they would be able to see us," said my father. "No. The best thing is to use the darkness to cover our approach. Our plan will be to sail round the island to Kilbricken quay. Then we can get the police after them."

"But what if they try to stop us?"

"We'll have to wait and see. We can make up our minds how to act when we see what they do."

We assembled our weapons, and a poor collection they were. We had the pick-axe, so kindly provided by Pat, but we did not want to use such a deadly weapon if it could be avoided. We each had a penknife, but none of them was very good.

"A stone in a stocking is a fine weapon," said Mike wistfully. "I wish we had brought some stones from the island."

But we had not done this, and it was no use lamenting over it now. Pat had taken Matt's knife, Sally, from me. She would have been useful now.

At last we cut up some wood into short thick pieces, with a handgrip whittled out. We would use these as clubs.

"If they use their guns we're finished," said my father. "I hope they will be afraid of rousing the people in the village."

It was another day before we sighted Fort Island. In the morning its long blue ridge rose out of the blue sea. When we got closer we could see the smaller islands stretching away to the west of it, and beyond them the high, clear mountains of the mainland. We gave a tremendous cheer at the sight of it, which sent our fishes scuttling away in fright. Then we hove to and lowered the sails.

It was wearisome waiting there in mid-ocean for night to fall. We talked little, for each of us felt a tension growing in him, because we had no way of knowing what lay ahead. We could see the white tower of the lighthouse, and we were sure that we must be observed by our enemies before evening.

"We can't help it if they see us," said my father. "In a way, perhaps it's as well if they do. If they try to wreck us by changing the lights, we'll be able to give evidence against them in court."

"If we're alive," was the thought in everyone's mind, but no one voiced it.

The boat needed very little attention, for there was only a little swell disturbing the surface of the sea. I got to thinking of my mother and Billy waiting at home for news of us, and I fingered my miserable weapons with determination to use them to the full.

Joe was the most silent of all. He always went dumb when danger threatened, but a fierce spirit burned inside him all the more furiously for that. He had induced a herring-gull to come down off the mast and settle on the gunwale. He murmured and whistled to him quietly, while the gull bowed and shifted from one big grey foot to the other. The gull spread his wings and circled the boat once, and came back again to the gunwale. Then they continued the conversation.

At last the evening began to come on. A single star appeared in a greenish sky, and a blue-grey haze lay on the sea. I shivered a little in the cool breeze, though my hands were hot and wet with excitement.

Still we waited. Darkness stole towards us over the water. Now we could hardly see Fort Island, except as a dim curved line in the sky. Still no light appeared.

"They'll wait till it's pitch dark," said Mike. "They always do that when they're wrecking."

"But don't people want to know why the lighthouse lamp is not lit at dusk?" I asked.

"That's the one drawback about their plan," said Mike. "They always have to let on that the lamp went out of order. We on the island don't believe that yarn, but it seems to satisfy other people. The islanders say: 'Rats always work best in the dark!' "

"I'm glad those two steamers got in ahead of us," said Joe.

Now it was so dark that we could not see the island at all.

The only lights showing were half a dozen dim points where Bunraha village was. Where the lighthouse should have been there was an ominous blackness. To the right of that we knew there was the long line of the cliffs. I remembered the jagged rocks at their feet where a boat could so easily be broken up.

Suddenly, as we watched, a light flared from the cliffs. It steadied, and remained like a wicked siren calling the ships to destruction.

"So that's how they do it!" Mike breathed excitedly. "The cleverness of them! They have their light fixed on a ledge of rock on the face of the cliff."

"How do you know?"

"That light is not high enough to be on the top of the cliff."

"That explains why the false light can never be seen from the island," said Joe.

"But an islander out in his boat could see it," said my father. "He'd know at once that it was a false light."

"There's their mistake," said Mike, rubbing his hands with delight. "I'd swear they never before put up a false light on a night of calm. They never get at their tricks until there is a howling wind and waves like mountains gone mad. Then all the islanders would be safe at home, they'd know, for not a man of them would risk his boat on a dirty night."

"Some island boat might come by at any moment," I said. "They certainly are taking a great risk for some treasure that may not exist at all, for all they know."

"I think I understand them," said my father.

He faced us all and looked us over seriously. Then he said quietly:

"Boys, I think we'll have to fight for our lives."

I said:

"But surely they would be afraid to kill us."

"Let me explain it like this," said my father. "The light-keepers and Pat have killed before—not directly, of course, but they have caused the deaths of sailors by wrecking ships. Don't think, then, that their consciences will trouble them much if they succeed in making an end of the four of us. They want the treasure, and they were always prepared to kill for it. How much more so now! Our deaths would make them safe. No one would ever hear that they locked up Joe in the tower, and that they intended to drown you all on the way home from the island. Now they have put up a false light to wreck us, but they can't risk one of us surviving to tell the tale."

We had no doubt that he was right. I could see that the very best thing they could do would be to finish us off silently. Dead men tell no tales. And how Matt would cry when he was explaining that in spite of him we went off by ourselves! We tricked him, we locked him up in Saint Kieran's cell. He got free, and Pat would tell how they met, and at great trouble managed to catch Joe. Joe was a bit unbalanced, poor fellow! But his friends released him, and they all went off together—three boys on the open Atlantic Ocean! What could you expect, he'd say. They probably foundered in the first blow of wind. And remember there was a bit of a storm not long after they left. The lost island? That's only a yarn. Pat could afford a little fun, and he didn't mind pleasing the boys by letting them do up the boat and go off for a few days with Matt to look after them. Look at the name they put on the boat—*Wave-Rider*! Could you beat that for a silly romantic idea? (I could see Pat's expression change to one of self-condemnation.) His conscience would never again be at peace. He would always remember how foolish he had been to gratify the boys' foolish longings. It was a terrible thing to feel that the deaths of three fine young lads lay at his own door. Then he would look solemn, and shake his head, and Matt standing beside him would let out a tear. And everyone would comfort them and tell them it was Fate, and we were going to die young anyway, and if Pat were not the instrument of our deaths, someone else would have to be. Then Pat would look noble, as one who carried the burdens of all the people on his own back. Presently he would convert the pearls and the white furs into cash, and settle down to an honourable old age.

My blood boiled at the thought of this. Joe and Mike had followed the same line of thought, and by their faces I guessed that they were not going to give in tamely. My father looked us over grimly.

"I can see you all agree with me," he said. He turned to Mike. "How many light-keepers are there?"

"Two," said Mike. "Then there will be Pat Conway and Matt."

"Four. All grown men. Are you sure the light-keepers won't have a few friends to help them?"

"There are never more than two," said Mike. "I'm sure of that."

"But we never told them we were really going to the island to find you, Mr. Farrell," said Joe. "We decided they would be more eager to help if they thought we were simply going after the treasure."

"So our party will be bigger than they expect," I finished.

"Good!" said my father. "Now we'll be able to surprise them. That's a valuable point in our favour. Still, if we can avoid a hand-to-hand fight, it will be far better. We'll keep to our plan of sailing to Kilbricken and getting the police to help. To work, now!"

I felt a tightness and a shivering all over me. I sprang to hoist the mainsail, but the work only partly relieved the tension. Mike stropped his penknife on the sole of his boot.

"Thumb on the blade and strike upwards," he said. "That's the best way always with a penknife. Ho-ho, boys! Just wait till I get after you!"

"You're a bloodthirsty fellow, to be sure," my father laughed. "I almost think you'll be sorry if we don't have to go to battle."

"Sorry I'll be, then," said Mike. "Though by the look of those light-keepers, I'd say they'd blunt my good penknife on me!"

We were making good headway now, with the water smacking on the bows and curling away in a phosphorescent wave like an arrow-point. We were steering straight for the light, but we intended to swing away to round the island when we would have come in close.

The darkness seemed to increase as we approached the island, and the lights of the village had gone out one by one. We carried no lights on the boat, of course. I judged that it must be well past midnight now. Nearer and nearer we came to the false light. We had to use it as a mark by which to set our course. Now we were only three hundred yards out from the cliffs.

Suddenly I knew what was going to happen.

"Turn away!" I shouted. "They'll be after us! They don't expect us to wreck on the rocks on a calm night—this trick of moving the light could only work on a stormy night!"

My father swung the helm hard over.

"What a fool I am! Start the engine! Hurry!"

I fumbled at the engine in the dark. How easily I could have had it ready in advance! Just then we all heard the tick-tick-tick of Pat's motor-boat. I paused for a second to listen. I tore at the engine. It coughed and died, twice, before I got it going. I raced it for all it was worth. But the efficient tick of Pat's boat was coming nearer every second.

"Lower the sails," shouted my father. "They'll capsize us if we can't attend to them."

But there wasn't time. I switched off the engine. A powerful searchlight had been lit on the bows of the motor-boat. It picked us out like a pointing finger, and in a moment the boat drew easily alongside us.

★ XIV ★

A boat-hook shot out, a line was thrown, and someone leaped on to our cabin roof. It was Matt. His little twisted form showed up stark against the searchlight as he made fast his line. It was done in a second. Then he was scrambling along the roof towards us. He dropped on to the deck.

Mike sprang on him and they started a silent battle. I rushed to help, but Mike panted:

"Another one! On the roof!"

A light-keeper this time, like a monkey. He dropped on to the deck too. I closed with him. His arms were like steel and his punch like a sledge-hammer. I whacked at him with my club and got him on the shoulder. He squealed and shot out a fist at me. It seemed to set my left ear on fire. I whacked again and missed, and then I jabbed with my club as if it were a dagger. I got him in the stomach, and knocked the wind out of him. But only for a second. He crouched back against the cabin door, knees bent, hands like claws. Suddenly there was a knife in his hand. He moved a step towards me, marking me as a weasel marks a rabbit He sprang. I hit out and got his wrist with my club, and turned the blade aside. But he had got me on the shoulder. He crouched back again. Out of the tail of my eye I could see my father wrestling with the other light-keeper on the roof.

The curious thing about all this was that not a word had been spoken. The boat rocked under our feet so that the water splashed against the sides. Our own heavy panting was the only other sound. The searchlight on the motor-boat's bows was pointed away from the scene of battle, but a sort of glow came backwards from it so that we could dimly see our opponents.

Now Mike grunted with satisfaction as Matt's body dropped on the deck. He paused only to shift his club a little in his hand before leaping on my light-keeper. He knocked the knife out of his hand while I brought my club down on his head. He fell and lay still. We stood there panting. Suddenly Mike shouted:

"Look out!"

We ducked just as the boom swung over. Now we saw that the two boats, still tied together, were drifting in to the cliffs. On the cabin roof, my father was still playing hide and seek with his man around the bale of furs. Mike leaped to the anchor, and it went rattling down into the water. I clambered on to the cabin roof and grasped the light-keeper by the ankle just as he dodged forward. He came crashing down on to the deck Mike hit him on the head, and there he lay.

"One, two, three!" said Mike triumphantly. "That's the lot, and I never used my good knife at all!"

"Just a moment, please," said a cool voice from the motor-boat.

The searchlight swung around and held us all in its beam. My father was standing on the cabin roof, backed by the bale of furs. Mike and I were on the deck below.

"The first one who moves will never move again," came the voice, Pat Conway's voice, from the motor-boat. "I'm a good shot, and I have my gun here in my hand."

He was in darkness, so that we could not see him, but we never doubted that he had the gun trained on us.

"You there on the roof, whoever you are," he went on. "Get down below with the others."

My father moved towards us. All at once I felt sick and dizzy. Where was Joe? I had forgotten him. Had he fallen overboard? Had Pat got him? I made a quick movement. Pat barked:

"Quiet, there, or I'll blow your head off!"

Plan after plan darted into my head. How stupid it was to have vanquished three of the gang, and to be held at bay, all three of us, by a single one. I thought of risking a jump for the other boat, but I discarded the idea. Pat would pick me off at his ease as I climbed aboard. It would be better to stay together, and make a concerted assault when we would get the chance.

My father paused on the verge of the cabin roof.

"You'll regret it if you shoot," he said, in a loud, clear voice.

"That's my concern," said Pat suavely. "I'm prepared to take a risk. Hurry, please! We've wasted enough time already."

Suddenly my father threw his arms in the air and shouted:

"Hit him, Joe!"

There was a thud, and the sound of the gun crashing on to the deck. Someone swung the light inwards, so that it showed Pat lying in a huddle on the deck of his own boat. Then came Joe's voice, waveringly:

"I—I think he's knocked out, all right, Mr. Farrell!"

Joe! Joe had done it all! The smallest, the timid one! He had crept away while we were fighting, guessing that Pat was on the motor-boat, waiting with his club in his hand to save all our lives with a timely wallop.

Mike and I danced with joy. Mike had taken his boots off before the fight, and now he hopped over in his bare feet into the other boat. He threw his arms round Joe and lifted him up in the air, and ran up and down the deck with him, uttering wild shouts, until poor Joe begged to be let down.

Now my father said:

"The job isn't finished yet. Some of these hard-headed lads may recover."

He set us all to tie their wrists and ankles with ropes, and to lay them all out like herrings on the deck of the *Wave-Rider*. He himself saw to the trussing-up of Pat. None of them was very badly injured, though they would all have headaches for a few days.

As for our own wounds, they were not very serious either. I had a gash on my shoulder from my man's knife, Mike's man had bitten his ear, and my father had a cut on his arm. We also had a fine collection of bruises, but we cared nothing for them.

Now we tied a tow-rope from the motor-boat to our own. We got our sails down at last, and then we tidied up the signs of our battle. Mike stayed on the *Wave-Rider* to steer her, while my father and Joe and I went in the motor-boat. We hauled in the anchor and started up the engine.

"What about the false light?" I said.

"The only way to that light is down the cliff from above," said Mike. "The moment we land, I'll run around the top of the cliff and put it out."

"But we must get the right light going again as soon as possible," said Joe. "That means landing on the lighthouse island first. And that will delay putting out the false light."

"I know what to do," said my father.

He picked up Pat's revolver, which still lay where he had dropped it. He took careful aim and fired. The light on the cliff flared and went out. The echoes went away and away and away from point to point of the cliffs, till they were gone.

Now we brought the motor-boat round in a slow curve, weighted down with the *Wave-Rider*. No one had suggested sailing our own boat in, for we were all very weary now, and there still remained much to be done.

We swung the searchlight so that its beam made a long path on which we travelled. It was not long till the light touched the long white wall of the lighthouse, and soon after we drew in to the little pier. Mike understood the light, and he and Joe landed to get it going again. My father and I waited in the boat. Presently the big beam was flashing on and off again, brightening the sky and the smooth sea all around it. A few minutes later Joe and Mike were on board again, and we were heading for Bunraha.

We had not gone more than a few hundred yards when our searchlight picked out a currach rowing vigorously towards us. Beyond that was another, which seemed to be trying to outdo the first one, and beyond that again were many more—too many for us to be able to count them. As they came nearer we saw that there were two men rowing each currach, and a few passengers as well. As they swung up and down on their oars they made an odd picture in the dimness.

Presently, above the sound of the motor-boat, we heard all the men singing together. Their voices travelled lightly from one boat to another in a deep, wild, rhythmic chorus. It was a song in Irish that I did not know, but it stirred my blood in some mysterious way. In between the verses, someone would give vent to a long cry, in which Mike joined. Soon we were surrounded by currachs. A voice came from the leading one:

"Hora, Mike!"

"Hoigh, Big Johnny!" Mike bellowed back.

A cheer rose from all the currachs, and then their song started up again. We slowed our pace so that the currachs could keep up with us, and they formed a guard of honour on either side. Now we could see Bunraha, and a great flaring bonfire lighting on the quay. Figures of women and children danced about it, the women's long skirts spread wide against the blaze. Every house in the village had a light streaming from its open door.

Soon we reached the quay. We threw up a line, and it was seized and tied up in a second. All the currachs crowded around us, and the men climbed from one to the other to land on the quay. Now at last the moment had come for us to step ashore.

Mike hopped out on his bare feet before any of us. A woman rushed from the crowd of watchers and scolded and blessed him all in one breath, while Big Johnny stood by, stiff with pride. The rest of us followed.

Big Johnny was big, even for a Fort Islander, where they have plenty of tall men. He towered head and shoulders over everyone there. He wore a bushy black beard, and he had the same bright dancing eye as Mike. The others seemed to regard him as a sort of leader, for they all fell silent when he began to speak.

"This is a great night for us. From where I stand now, I can see four black-hearted criminals tied up like little cocks going to the market, and they lying in a neat row on the boat's floor. That's a thing we have been waiting for, for a long time, and I'm only sorry we didn't have the pleasure of doing it ourselves."

The crowd cheered, and then Big Johnny went on:

"Now it's after midnight, and time for all respectable people to be going to bed. But *I'm* not going to bed! And *you're* not going to bed! We're all going up to my house, and we'll have eating and drinking and *céilí* till morning!"

Again the crowd broke into cheers. Suddenly, they stopped. A woman had darted forward into the flare of the fire, a red-haired woman, small and fat.

"To *your* house, is it, Big Johnny?" she said sweetly. "And would you tell me now, why would we all go to *your* house?"

"Because—because my son, Mike has come back," Big Johnny spluttered.

"Is that all?" She pulled me forward. "Come here, young boy, and tell me did you ever see me before?"

She put her chin in the air, so that I could see her better.

"You're Sally Rua MacDonagh," I said, smiling.

"Who held Pat Conway in talk while you hid in the hen-house?"

"You did."

"Who sent Big Johnny over to the light-keepers with a present of lovely whiskey, while you got away in the currach? Who got you the currach? Who gave you a feather-bed to sleep on while you waited till it was time to go?"

"You did."

She turned to the crowd and called out:

"Whose house will you go to to-night, where there's wine and punch on the table for all, and soda-cake and currant-cake, and a feast for everyone? Who heard the shot fired? Who saw the light go on? Who told you all to take out the currachs and go out to meet the heroes coming home?"

"Sally Rua! Sally Rua! We'll go to Sally's!" they all shouted.

But Sally wasn't finished. She turned to Big Johnny and said contemptuously:

"And you're the man that wouldn't let me into one of the currachs, after all I had done! Bah!"

Big Johnny shrugged good-humouredly.

"Women and rabbits should never be let into a boat," he said. "They bring bad luck."

Everyone burst out laughing, and then we all started up the hill to Sally's house, leaving a man to guard the boat, with its prisoners.

We were made to go in front, with Sally and Big Johnny

and his wife, who were all the best of friends in spite of the argument. As many as possible crowded into the house, while the rest stayed around the door. In a few minutes, Sally had a glass and a slice of cake in everyone's hand, inside and out. Then our wounds were bandaged and wondered over, and after that my father had to tell the story of his adventures.

Somehow all our weariness had left us. We sat on there in the kitchen until someone brought out a melodeon. Then everyone moved outside and began to dance in the little sandy square between the houses, lit by the lights from the open doors. They danced sets and reels until the early dawn broke. The islanders were tireless. They would have gone on for hours more. But we had had a lively night, and we had a long day's sailing before us. Sally said we must all stay with her, but as she only had one big bed for us, she had to let Joe go with Big Johnny.

Just as everyone was about to go home, a side-car clattered into the village. The big sergeant sat on the side, and Ned, the policeman, was on the box. Someone had gone to Kilbricken with the story of the capture of Pat and Matt and the light-keepers.

"Show them to us! We'll take them away at once!" said Ned fiercely. "That little fellow walked on my wall-flowers!"

Everyone stayed to see the four prisoners hoisted on to the side-car. Their heads were heavy, and they implored Ned not to drive too fast. I felt quite sorry for Pat Conway. Without him, we could not have gone to the lost island at all. I resolved that when he would come out of gaol—for to gaol they would all certainly go for their wrecking activities—I would pay my debt to him of half the value of the furs and the pearls. Perhaps they would set him up in some respectable business, though I could not imagine Pat taking to this idea.

SEAN O'CONNELL

It was high noon before we woke from our sleep. When we had breakfasted, we went down to the quay, escorted by the whole village. The men had our boat ready, for many of them seemed not to have gone to bed at all. We were to leave the motor-boat at the quay, for the police to collect later on.

We had to shake every man's hand and promise to come again to visit them, before we were allowed to embark. Mike made us name the very day we would come. At last, however, our sails were up, and we were headed out to sea.

Our course lay along the length of the island. It was a pleasant day of sun, but with a good strong breeze, so that we made good time. Still, when we were passing the cliffs, a crowd of islanders had already arrived there, and they cheered and waved until we could see them no more.

We passed Kilkieran, where we had imprisoned Matt, and we told my father the details of the story that we had forgotten up to now. As we reached the head of the bay, we saw the passenger steamer on its way in to Kilbricken. We knew there would be tremendous excitement in the village. It was not every day that four desperate criminals had to be marched on board the steamer.

It was wonderful to watch my father picking out the places on either side of the bay, as we sailed the long way in. He named mountain villages, cliffs and harbours that Joe and I could barely distinguish in the blue haze. He tried to sit still by the helm, but he could not. He was forever darting forward to examine one or other well-known landmark, and marvelling that it had remained in position all the time that he had been away. At last Joe and I took over the management of the boat ourselves, and he went to gaze ahead at the approaching town, as if he would drag it towards him with his hungry eyes.

It was late evening, and the fishing-boats were beginning to steal out of the docks under their black sails, when we reached the town. Joe steered us expertly between the buoys, until at last we lowered our sails and glided along the dock-side, before Pete's door. That was a moment of solemn joy.

The lamps were beginning to show in the houses. Joe made the boat fast, and went at once to open his own door. A moment later Mrs. Pete was rushing out to us, laughing and crying and thanking heaven for our safe return, all in one breath.

"I never expected to see you again," she said.

But there we were. We spent a few minutes in telling our adventures briefly, while Joe went to borrow a horse and trap from a neighbour. We left the boat and its cargo in charge of Joe, for disposing of the furs and the pearls would be work for another day. Not long afterwards my father and I were on our way out of the town.

I was like to burst with pride as I watched him. The horse was a good one, and the trap new and well-sprung. Neither of us spoke, except when I said it looked as if we would get home before dark. He made no answer, but looked longingly ahead at the road.

At last we turned into our lane. The horse's hooves moved silently on the sand, and then we heard my mother's voice, high and melodious, calling her hens to come home. We turned into the farmyard, and there she was at the door. We climbed down out of the trap, and then we all went into the house together.

EILÍS DILLON (1920–1994) wrote more than thirty books for young people, as well as fiction for adults, including the best-selling historical novel *Across the Bitter Sea*, about the struggle for Irish independence in the nineteenth and twentieth centuries. With few exceptions, her young people's books are set in the west of Ireland, in small communities struggling to make a living on the islands and along the Atlantic coast. As the critic Declan Kiberd wrote in Dillon's obituary: "What Laura Ingalls Wilder did for children's literature in the US, she achieved in Ireland, imparting a sure historical sense in books such as *The Singing Cave.* That interest in history was a natural expression of her curiosity of mind, and of her family inheritance."

Building on a family tradition of agitation for Irish independence (her mother's brother was one of seven men who signed the Proclamation of the Irish Republic and was executed by the British at the end of the 1916 Easter Rising), Eilís Dillon committed herself to preserving and promoting Irish literature and culture. She was a Fellow of the Royal Society of Literature and a member and strong supporter of Aosdána, the national association of writers, artists, and composers. She even wrote a few of her children's books in Gaelic, the native Irish language. But, as Kiberd explains, "There was nothing narrowly provincial in her writing: she simply assumed that books about children in Irish settings, if properly written, would be of universal appeal. And so they have proved to be."

RICHARD KENNEDY (1910–1989) illustrated several of Eilís Dillon's books for children. In addition to collaborating on the early design of Puffin Books, Kennedy provided illustrations for several of the press's most celebrated writers, including J. M. Barrie (creator of Peter Pan) and Astrid Lindgren (creator of Pippi Longstocking). His illustrated memoir of working with Leonard and Virginia Woolf in the 1920s was published as *A Boy at the Hogarth Press*.

TITLES IN THE NEW YORK REVIEW
CHILDREN'S COLLECTION

ESTHER AVERILL
Captains of the City Streets
The Hotel Cat
Jenny and the Cat Club
Jenny Goes to Sea
Jenny's Birthday Book
Jenny's Moonlight Adventure
The School for Cats

DINO BUZZATI
The Bears' Famous Invasion of Sicily

EILÍS DILLON
The Island of Horses
The Lost Island

ELEANOR FARJEON
The Little Bookroom

RUMER GODDEN
An Episode of Sparrows

MUNRO LEAF AND ROBERT LAWSON
Wee Gillis

NORMAN LINDSAY
The Magic Pudding

ERIC LINKLATER
The Wind on the Moon

E. NESBIT
The House of Arden

BARBARA SLEIGH
Carbonel: The King of the Cats

T.H. WHITE
Mistress Masham's Repose

REINER ZIMNIK
The Bear and the People
The Crane